DRAGON'S TORMENT

BADLANDS PARANORMAL POLICE DEPARTMENT:
BOOK ONE

JOHN P. LOGSDON

ORLANDO A. SANCHEZ

CRIMSON MYTH
PRESS

© 2018 by John P. Logsdon & Orlando A. Sanchez

Published by: Crimson Myth Press (www.CrimsonMyth.com)

Cover Art: Audrey Logsdon (www.AudreyLogsdon.com)

Thanks to TEAM ASS!
Advanced Story Squad

This is the first line of readers of the series. Their job is to help us keep things in check and also to make sure we're not doing anything way off base in the various story locations!

(listed in alphabetical order by first name)

Adam Saunders-Pederick
Bennah Phelps
Debbie Tily
Hal Bass
Helen Saunders-Pederick
Ian Nick Tarry
Jamie Gray
Jan Gray
Janice Kelly
Jodie Stackowiak
John Debnam
Kevin Frost
Larry Diaz Tushman
Marie McCraney
Megan McBrien
Mike Helas
Natalie Fallon
Paulette Kilgore
Penny Campbell-Myhill

Sandy Lloyd
Scott Reid
Sharon Harradine
Tehrene Hart

Thanks to Team DAMN
Demented And Magnificently Naughty

This crew is the second line of readers who get the final draft of the story, report any issues they find, and do their best to inflate our fragile egos.

(listed in alphabetical order by first name)

Adam Goldstein, Alan Robert Bruce, Allen Stark, Amy Robertson, Angie Hill, Anne Morando, Audrey Cienki, Barbara Henninger, Beth Adams, Bethany Olsen, Bonnie Dale Keck, Carol Evans, Carolyn Fielding, Cat, Chris Christman II, Cindy D., Corinne Loder, Dana Audette, Darren Musson, David Botell, Denise King, Dorothy Phillips, Emma Porter, Helen Day, Ingrid Schijven, Jacky Oxley, Jeem, Jen Cooper, Jen Stubbs, Jeremy, John Rayner, Julie Peckett, Karen Hollyhead, Kathleen Portig, Laura Cadger Rogers, Laura Tallman, LeAnne Benson, Lindsay Stroven, Marc, Mary Letton, MaryAnn Sims, Melanie Groves VonFange, Melissa Parsons, Michelle Reopel, Myles, Penny Noble, Ramsey Freiland, Sara Mason Branson, Scott Ackerman, Sharon Harradine, Stacey Stein, Steve Winder, Susan Prentice, Terri Adkisson, Tony Dawson, Wanda Corder-Jones, Wendy Schindler, Zak Klepek.

CHAPTER 1

*N*o good deed goes unpunished.

"We don't get many dragons in here," the troll said, giving me the once over. His bass voice reverberated in the spacious bar. "What'll it be?"

I looked up at the hulking figure behind the smooth bar counter and paused. Most trolls were large. This one took it to the next level. Contrary to the myths, they didn't live under bridges, and they were incredibly intelligent. The part about smashing you to a pulp and ripping off your arms was pretty spot on though.

After a day of the mind-numbing paperwork that my new position required, I walked into *The Dirty Goblin* searching for a moment of peace and a warm glass of good blood ale.

Both of which were usually an impossible find in the Badlands.

"How did you—?" I started when he raised a tree trunk arm and pointed to his eyes. I looked across the bar into the mirror and saw my reflection.

"Shit," I said, patting my pockets.

I'd forgotten my glasses at PPD Headquarters. A few seconds later, I found my backup pair and put them on, hiding my eyes. The fact that my irises were vertical slits was a clear indicator of what I truly was.

There was a time when dragons went around eating everything and everyone in sight. Dragons didn't do that anymore—unless provoked. But we still weren't exactly loved. More loved than hellions, but what wasn't? Satyrs, I guess, but they took the term 'love' a bit more literally.

"New in town?" he asked, his rough voice filled the empty bar, bouncing off the wall. "You don't look like a tourist."

"The Badlands don't get tourists," I countered.

He nodded and laughed. "Not if they want to stay alive."

"You carry blood ale?" I asked, parking at the far end of the bar and dropping a pile of papers on the wood counter, worn smooth by years of use. "The real kind, not that commercial energy drink piss."

"We have home-brewed blood ale and valkyrie rations," the troll answered. "You want something edible, you'll need to go elsewhere."

"You have a valkyrie cook?" I jolted, looking around. "No wonder this place is empty. Did she kill everyone?"

"Only the first handful," he grunted. "Now it's mostly food poisoning."

I shuddered at the thought of V-rations. "Just the blood ale, thanks."

The troll nodded and placed a tall glass of the deep red ale on the bar. I reached for it and he held the glass in place with one massive hand, while pointing to a sign with the other.

It read:

No Weapons-No Trouble
No Compliance-Know Pain
Let Percy keep you and your weapons safe.
Failure to do so will result in extreme ejection from the premises.

"I'll relieve you of those hand-cannons, please." Percy pointed to the top of the bar. "Slow."

The Twins, as I referred to them, Pinky and Butterfly, were custom-made Fossberg 590 Tactical Shockwave shotguns. They were technically firearms since the barrel length was less than eighteen inches and had pistol grips. I just knew they were the perfect conversation enders, especially when bullets were flying my way.

When a troll requests your weapons, it's usually best to comply. This troll had requested my shotguns *before* serving the blood ale.

Smart.

I opened my coat and slowly pulled my lovelies from the shoulder holsters.

"You have sharp eyes."

"The sharpest," the troll answered. "Besides, those things aren't exactly what I would call subtle."

Trolls dismantled most arguments, usually starting with the person doing the arguing.

In the spirit of diplomacy and keeping my arms

attached, I placed my custom-made shotguns slowly on the bar, butt first.

He slid the glass my way without spilling a drop.

"I'm going to go out on a limb here"—I slid my weapons over before grabbing the glass—"Percy?"

He nodded, placing my shotguns behind the bar.

"Owner and operator of this wonderful establishment" —he swept an arm around the bar—"and you are?"

"Ezekias," I said, raising the glass, taking a sip, and nodding in approval. It was good. "Most call me Zeke."

Percy must've seen my expression. "Good?"

"Excellent, haven't had home-brewed blood ale since I was home."

"Didn't know dragons enjoyed blood ale, usually it's valkyries drinking it like water." Percy gave me a friendly smile. Either that or he had gas. It was tough to tell the difference with trolls. "Enjoy," he added before moving off to the other end of the bar.

I took a long pull of the warm blood ale. The hammer and chisel headache trying to carve out my brain settled down to a dull thudding sensation.

Hazy warmth wrapped itself around me.

I spread out the files and made the counter into a makeshift desk.

My hand reflexively dropped to my side to rest on the butt of my shotgun before I remembered Percy's 'no weapons' policy.

I looked at the files in front of me, cursed my life and my mother. I didn't dare say her name out loud, though. Valkyries have been known to have exceptional hearing. She'd kick my ass all over the Badlands if I invoked a curse in her name. Hilda the Terror earned her title the old-fashioned way—by the number of dead bodies left in her wake.

I took a long drag of the blood ale and shook my head examining the files.

My team, if you could call it that, consisted of a hellion named Rose, a demonoid, some sort of void/demon hybrid named Graffon; Doe, a faceless, a.k.a. Void; Nimble, a slug; Silk, a dark fae; and a—I rubbed my eyes to make sure I read the file correctly—a malkyrie named Butch?

That last one had to be a typo.

This wasn't a team.

It was a disaster of epic proportions.

I'd like to meet the genius who thought a dragon chief with a hellion second-in-command was a good idea. That right there was a recipe for assassination. Dragons and hellions weren't exactly known for getting along.

Hell, the fact was that the Badlands Paranormal Police Department had been built on tape and bubblegum. Three major factions had to be represented. Dragons, hellions, and hell. The dragons and hellions' part was easy, but hell consisted of many races, from goblins to satyrs to manticores to valkyries…the list went on and on.

The Badlands PPD went through chiefs faster than a dragon devoured normals. Again, they didn't really do that any more. Not by choice, exactly, but it was still off limits. That was because topside was a big no-no to people living in the Badlands.

After a chief bit the dust, the next in line jumped in on rotation. So, if a hellion died, a representative from hell was the new chief. Once that one got obliterated, a dragon was sworn in. After the dragon, it was back to the hellion, and the wheel started spinning yet again.

The problem was that most of the time the cops just shot each other.

Fastest way to the top, even if it only lasted a couple days.

People living in the Badlands weren't exactly known for the long view.

I massaged my temples and noted the exits around me. Old habit. At least *The Dirty Goblin* was quiet and empty. Percy, who was large enough to have his own gravitational field, probably scared anyone who wasn't suicidal or a regular.

I took another sip of blood ale and sorted the paperwork in front of me. My first gut reaction was to incinerate the paperwork and maybe the bar with it.

We didn't do that anymore either.

Hilda's words came back to me.

"You're a warrior," she said, sharpening her blade. "This will be good training for you. You need to get out into the world. Learn what it means to lead others in battle."

"I'm a dragon, not a babysitter. What does a PPD chief do anyway?"

"You'll bring order to the Badlands."

"Order to the Badlands? That sentence has so much wrong with it I don't know where to begin. I'm a warrior, raised by warriors. Not a cop. PPD chiefs do not lead others in battle. They shuffle paper and deal with pains in the ass. There's nothing glorious in that."

"You are a colossal pain in my ass, Ezekias. You will take

this assignment and do it with honor. Perhaps you will not lead your people in battle, but this is the Badlands. Anything is possible."

"I still think this is a bad—"

"This conversation is over."

She placed the blade on the table between us, daring me to contradict her.

I chose a strategic retreat and accepted the position of PPD Chief.

Hilda the Terror wasn't known for her gentle parenting skills.

Other children received warm cuddles and hugs. Valkyrie children usually got slashes, bruises, and stitches. My first 'toy' was a doubled-edged short sword named Gash. I nearly cut off my fingers the first time I used it.

Hilda's reputation came from her sword skills on the battlefield and the food of her kitchen. She had produced a staggering amount of fatalities in both areas. Her culinary skills left much to be desired, like a swift decapitation or maybe an evisceration. Valkyries weren't known for their expertise with food. That probably explained the shortage of valkyrie chefs.

The blood ale haze had settled into a comfortable glow.

It was in these moments that the Badlands almost felt peaceful.

If you fell for the illusion, they usually found your body, or what was left of it, in some back alley of Infernal City.

Yes, the Badlands was a voracious mistress. She

chewed you up and spat you out, all the while caressing your neck and slitting your throat.

"There's no place like home," I mumbled.

At least it was calm and peaceful right now. The only thing that would make it even better would be another mug of homebrew.

I was just about to ask Percy for a refill when a body crashed through the window.

CHAPTER 2

*T*he plate glass window shattered from the impact, sending ballistic shards in every direction, and forcing me to duck. The body that decided to renovate the façade slammed into the bar with a sick thud, sliding down the other side.

Blood and my drink spilled everywhere.

So much for a quiet moment.

"Angry customers?" I asked, wiping off my jacket while looking at Percy.

He pushed the body away with his massive foot.

"All my customers are angry," Percy answered, grabbing a gun. "Badlands, remember?"

He had a point.

Anyone with half a brain knew this job came with trouble, but I didn't expect it to greet me on the first day.

I heard the guns cock and dove behind the bar as bullets tore into the wood, shredding the stool I had occupied seconds earlier.

Whoever launched the dead guy into *The Dirty Goblin*

was just warming up. The body was just the start of the conversation. I needed to speak a language they understood.

"I need Pinky," I hollered over the gunfire. "Give it to me, now."

"Who?" Percy asked, keeping low as the gunmen shattered bottles above his head. "There's no one here by that name."

"My weapon." I held out my hand. "Hand me Pinky."

He furrowed his brow at me.

"Pinky," I barked at him. "Now!"

Like a first year recruit, he jolted and reached under the counter, handing me a shotgun. I fired over the edge of the bar and shook my head.

"That's Butterfly," I growled, tossing Percy the shotgun. "Hand me Pinky!"

"There's a difference?" He handed me the other shotgun. "They look identical to me."

I fired over the bar and waited a few seconds.

"You probably want to hold on to something," I warned, bracing myself against the bar. "Make sure you stay down."

"Why? That one fired just like the last—"

The shockwave *thwumped* outside of the bar and rushed into *The Dirty Goblin*, shattering the remaining windows. A wall of flame followed the shockwave, racing over our heads and across the bar.

It was a beautiful sight.

I admired the flames as they roared above us—it's a dragon thing.

"Dragon rounds," I said, patting Pinky as more gunfire

erupted across the bar. "Pass me Butterfly. I don't think they're done."

I stayed down and fired Butterfly over the bar. For a split second, I thought about going dragon. I must've been tired. The broken glass and damage could be repaired. If I went dragon, *The Dirty Goblin* would become a dirty crater, and I was really enjoying the homebrewed ale. I couldn't go full dragon anyway. My tattoo stopped that from happening. Still, I could dragon it up enough to ruin Percy's chance at only dealing with non-structural damage.

I glanced over at the body that had interrupted my drink. If he wasn't dead on impact, the several bullet holes in him convinced me he was gone now.

"Anyone you know?" I asked, turning him over. "Seems well dressed for this part of the city."

"Hellion diplomat or businessman," Percy answered. "Not used to seeing that in this part of town. Probably looking for something hard, fast, and fun."

"Looks like he found the hard and fast part." I reached into his pocket and pulled his wallet. "Shit, diplomat from House Mal."

"House Malevolent?" Percy asked, looking more skittish than a troll ever should. "This is bad."

This hellion diplomat just transformed my situation from bad to clusterfuck.

"Why don't you call your team?" Percy asked, returning fire.

"My team?"

"You're PPD right? Maybe you should call backup?"

"How did you—?" I said, reloading Butterfly.

Pinky was going to take a while before I could fire it again. Dragon rounds were great at clearing out an area, but couldn't be fired in rapid succession.

"Saw the files you were reading. PPD logo on top."

"Sharp eyes," I said with a nod. "Yes, I'm PPD."

"I think now might be a good time to call them."

"They implanted this thing," I replied. "Give me a sec."

I wasn't a fan of having my brain messed around with, but part of the deal in joining the force was getting a connector. A slug by the name of Nimble hooked it all up. He was the tech guy in the Badlands PPD. He also gave me the standard-issue PPD tattoo, though he'd said that there were a few extras that had been requested be drawn in.

I wasn't one who read slugs all that well, but I would have guessed he seemed perplexed by the additional lines on my new tat. He put in a quick call, gave me as concerned a look as a slug could manage, and then got the drawing done.

"Rowena?" I called in through the connector, still not all that comfortable with it. *"Come in, Rowena!"*

Rowena was the Badlands Artificial Intelligence dispatcher.

A haughty cough came over my connector.

"Are you addressing me, Chief Phoenix?"

"Who the hell else would I be addressing?" I asked, as more gunfire tore into the bar.

"Excuse me? Is that attitude I hear? Please re-engage when you learn to conduct yourself like a civilized dragon, not some uncouth beast. The nerve."

"Shit, I'm forgetting something," I muttered to myself.

"Is your connector thing broken?" Percy asked. "Do you need a manual?"

I glared at him. "I got this, thanks."

Nimble had given me specific instructions. It was just a little difficult to concentrate with bullets trying to perforate me. His words came back to me.

"When you use the AI, make sure you use the title."

"Title?"

"Rowena," he said, wistfully, *"is the Badlands Intelligent Artificial Tactical Command Hub."*

"BIATCH? That's the title?"

"No!" Nimble yelled. *"You must never use that name with her. She will become furious."*

He'd scooted backward as if in fear. There was a small puddle of slug slime where he'd been. Was he so afraid of Rowena that he'd just...

No, I didn't want to think about that.

"Right," I'd replied. *"So, what do I call her?"*

"There was a slight...glitch with the programming code. Rowena thinks she's royalty. You have to call her Lady Rowena or she won't respond."

"Lady Rowena? You've got to be kidding."

"Remember, Lady Rowena."

I took a breath and tried to compose myself as bullets destroyed the bar.

"Hey, Zeke?" Percy asked. "I don't want to intrude on your private moment, but do you think you could stop these idiots *before* they completely destroy my bar?"

I raised a finger. "Got it now...I think."

"Rowena?" I tried, this time in a more cordial tone. *"Lady Rowena?"*

"Why, yes dear?"

I flipped open the auditory feed so she could hear what I was hearing.

"Do you happen to hear the gunfire in the background?"

"Of course. My auditory capacity far exceeds that of any dragon. It appears you've angered someone."

"You could say that."

"From the amount of projectiles impacting the surfaces, I'd say you've made some determined enemies on your first day. Congratulations, Chief Phoenix."

"Thank you," I replied tightly. *"I need help. Get Rose and the other teams to my location."*

"Which is?"

"What do you mean? You can track me, right?"

"Track you?" It was almost a shriek. *"Track you? I'm a sophisticated Artificial Intelligence. Emphasis on the art. Do you understand with whom you're speaking?"*

"An...artiste?"

"Precisely. Keep that in mind when you address me."

"So you can't track me?"

"Of course, but I don't do menial work like—tracking." She paused. *"Just tell me where you are. I'm certain it's one of those common establishments frequented by the dreck."*

I took a breath and fired Pinky again over the bar. Percy and I ducked under another wall of flame. The gunfire erupted a few seconds later.

"Persistent buggers," I said, reloading Butterfly and putting Pinky to the side.

"Company men," Percy answered. "Seems like you've pissed somebody off."

"Me?" I blurted. "I just got here. I haven't even had

time to piss anyone off." A bottle shattered on the back wall. "Maybe one of them ate the V-rations?"

"No way would they be up and about," Percy argued back, shaking his head. "What did you say you did at the PPD?"

"I didn't."

"Sounds like a chief," Percy said with a nod. "Consider this your official Infernal City welcome."

"I think I'd prefer the V-rations."

"They'd probably kill you faster."

"Lady Rowena," I said through the connector, *"I'm at The Dirty Goblin."*

"Aren't they all? Filthy creatures."

"Rowe—Lady Rowena. The name of the bar is the filth—The Dirty Goblin."

"The bar located near the end of the Strip?"

"Yes."

"Why didn't you say so? I'll inform the rest of the team. Should they bring a body bag? Are you injured?"

"No. Not as far as I can tell."

"Pity."

She ended the call.

I needed to find out who wanted to retire me so soon into my career.

I reached out with my senses and drew a blank. Someone was using energy signature dampeners, which meant money and power. ESD's weren't cheap or easy to come by.

Normally, they would work against most supernaturals, but I was a dragon.

This was a speed bump for me. I could get around

them but it meant unleashing power that I didn't feel all that comfy parting with.

I didn't have a choice. I needed to know who was doing the ballistic renovation of *The Dirty Goblin*.

"Shit," I mumbled.

"Shit?"

I nodded, giving Percy a look that let him know I was about to get naughty.

"Shit," he groaned, a wince appearing on his face.

I took a breath and unleashed my power.

CHAPTER 3

*D*ragons have several forms.

The tattoos given to me by the PPD gave me the ability to control precisely how far I transformed into my dragon form, which was a good thing. No one wanted a fully transformed dragon roaming the city. Aside from probably starting a war, there wouldn't be much of the city left. Regular dragons were in human form or dragon form—there was no in between, unless you were an advanced dragon…then you had some pretty decent control. I wasn't that advanced, so the PPD tattoo, mixed with the magic ring I wore—*Whoosh*—gave me the ability to control how far I changed.

I expanded my awareness and let my senses flow.

The smells hit me first. Gunpowder, blood, wood, alcohol, sweat, and fear. The last one made me smile.

I counted ten goblins outside the bar. They were focused on unloading as many bullets as possible into *The Dirty Goblin*.

"I'm going to need you to cover me," I instructed Percy, making sure Pinky and Butterfly were fully loaded.

"Cover you?" Percy asked, ducking behind the bar as a barrage of bullets flew overhead. "I know dragons are tough, but you aren't bulletproof. You go out there, Zeke, and the only cover you'll get is a sheet over your body."

Dragons in general were strong. We weren't as fast as hellions, but we could hold our own against a troll. Even though I couldn't go full dragon in this situation, the tattoo let me go half-dragon. In terms of power, a half-dragon beat a full anything most of the time.

"Give me a second, Percy," I said, taking off my glasses. "I think you'll feel differently once I'm done."

I hadn't had much time to practice this particular changeover ability, but I knew what it took to go full dragon. Get madder than hell, channel it, and feel the burn. Nimble told me that going partial dragon was the same idea, but instead of getting madder than hell, I should just get a bit annoyed. Clearly, Nimble didn't know me very well yet.

The world faded as I focused in and allowed the rage to well up inside me. I had to control it, obviously, but knowing how far was the trick.

Fortunately, I could sense the changes in my mind and body almost instantly.

Whenever in full dragon form, my sense of empathy disappeared. I became hungry, easily agitated, full of hate, and more paranoid than a guy bearing witness against the mob.

So, I had to hold back.

The best way for me to manage this was to get to the point where my empathy started to fade, and stop the transition.

I opened my eyes to find Percy was staring at me slack-jawed.

"Damn, dude," he breathed as the bullets continued peppering the area, "you look freaky as shit."

"Thanks."

"Are those scales?" he asked, reaching out as if unable to control himself from touching my face.

I slapped his hand away, jolting him back to the reality that he was dangerously close to seeing how it would feel to fight a partial dragon.

He blinked a few times.

"Uh...sorry."

"No problem," I grumbled. "Cover me."

He looked a bit panicked. "With what?"

"You don't have a weapon of your own back here?"

"Never needed one," he replied. "I kind of *am* a weapon."

"Not against bullets," I pointed out. Then, I started scanning the area, thinking that he probably was bulletproof, since he was made of rock. "Those bottles," I said quickly, "use them."

"For what?" he asked, frowning. "I don't get drunk that easily and those are tiny bottles compared to—"

"I want you to throw them at the goblins, Percy," I interrupted.

"Oh...oh!" He shook his head. "That's like a thousand bucks, Zeke."

"Which will do you no good if you're dead, Percy."

He opened his mouth as if to retaliate, but slowly closed it.

"Good point," he said, finally.

After he'd picked up a handful of munitions, he whimpered slightly, sighed, and then gave me a nod.

It was go time.

I leapt over the bar as Percy rose and launched the bottles into the street. Now, you may not think this would have been a big deal, being that they were just bottles, but that only means that you've never seen a troll launching bottles. It looked like he was hammering grenades at them.

One of the goblins got struck square in the chest. The poor bastard hadn't even had the time to scream. The bottle tore right into him, sticking slightly out of his person as he lay on his back with dead eyes.

It damn near made me wish I'd gone completely past the retainment of empathy.

The goblins immediately started taking cover behind their vehicles.

I ran to the first car and shoved it with my foot. It slid back and crushed three goblins.

Their screams filled the night.

It was a good sound.

Two goblins leapt at me, I turned and fired Butterfly, spraying little bits of goblin all over the street.

Two more down.

I slid over the hood of the closest car and landed in a roll as bullets chewed up the ground where I had stood moments earlier.

Five goblins left.

A bottle thudded and I heard the sound of a body slump to the ground.

Four goblins left.

The remaining creeps were behind a small truck, taking turns darting out from their cover to generously spray the car I was using as my shield with bullets.

I rolled to the rear of the car, took aim at the truck, and unleashed Pinky.

Then, I ran.

Something smacked against the back of my head, launching me forward into a roll. It hurt like hell, but I knew it wasn't a bullet.

"Sorry!" I heard Percy call from within the bar. "My bad!"

Damn trolls.

I cozied up to a wall and snapped up the unbroken bottle Percy had tagged me with. Homebrew. Considering what I was about to do, taking a quick swig was not a bad idea. Too bad my current form didn't understand the concept of sipping.

The bottle was empty in seconds.

It tasted just as good, but there would be no effect from the alcohol. Dragons didn't get blistered when out of human form.

I stood up and staggered.

Ah, yes. I wasn't fully in dragon form, which really sucked because my body wasn't processing the booze as if I were fully turned. Worse, when a dragon was only partially turned, booze hit fast. *Real* fast. This meant that I was going to be as drunk as a skunk in seconds.

Okay, so drinking a full bottle of homebrewed blood ale was probably *not* the best idea.

"All right, you bathtardth," I called out as the world began to swim. "I'm gonna give...*hic*...you todacounnaten to...*hic*...put down yer wea...*hic*...wea...*hic*...guns."

There was no response.

"One...two...uhhh..."

"Three," called out one of the goblins.

"Right, three," I yelled back. "Thanks, pal!"

I heard another goblin chastise Mr. Helper, saying, "Why are you helping him, idiot?"

"What?" he replied.

"Four...five...*hic*...six...seven."

I began to giggle at this point. I don't know why, but the word 'seven' sounded funny to me for some reason.

"Eigggggghhhht."

Now, I was singing the count.

"Niiiiiine...*hic*."

Bullets started flying my way. The goblins clearly did not want me to reach ten.

"*Hic*...ten!"

Firing more than one dragon round was taking a risk, and it wasn't possible with my shotgun setup. However, the distance I'd morphed had give me a buttload of strength. Translation: I could throw a dragon round with enough force to make it explode. It was a bad idea, sure, but even if I hadn't been in a drunken stupor, I'd have done it.

The dumber part of my plan was to stand up and laugh as I unleashed hell.

I threw the first round and watched as it blasted the truck into the air, blowing me back against the wall with a thud. If my scales hadn't been up, I'd have been incinerated.

"Jeez, Zeke," Percy hollered. "Could you warn a guy first?"

"What?" I yelled back. "I counted to...*hic*...ten!"

Clearly, the truck had taken the brunt of the heat, because the goblins were standing about twenty feet back from where it had been. The surprised expressions on their faces was priceless, but it was short-lived.

I grinned, waved, and fired round number two, this time from my shotgun.

It landed right in front of them and vaporized the group.

Two seconds later, the truck that had launched into the air landed, adding a finishing touch to the destruction by exploding.

I smacked the wall again.

Percy barked, "Damn it, Zeke!"

"What? I didn't know the...*hic*...truck wasgonnablowup."

Okay, I seriously needed to clear this booze from my system. With a firm focus, I channeled the rage a bit more, killing the alcohol completely and nearly doubling my size in the process. Then, I released all the energy and returned back to my human form.

When I snapped my eyes open, clarity was back on my side.

That's when I heard tires screeching behind me.

Three vehicles slid to a stop and boxed me in.

They were original prototype Hurricanes, used by Lamborghini to create their version. As usual, we'd provided the tech and the designs to the normals topside and they would marvel at the engineering genius. The Hurricanes were matte black automotive beasts with tinted windows and silver alloy rims. There were few vehicles in the Badlands that could outrun the PPD in those things.

I made an internal note of the time. It took them two minutes and thirty seconds from the moment I spoke to Rowena requesting backup until they appeared. It was an excellent response time, but it needed work.

I leapt across the hood of the car I used for cover and walked over to the burning wreck of the truck. Fire never bothered me. Dragons were pretty much flameproof, after all. I scanned the wreckage, making sure there weren't any goblin survivors before turning to the cars behind me.

The driver's side door of the center PPD vehicle opened and I found myself facing the barrels of two Smith & Wesson .500's. Good choice. If I hadn't had the Twins, those would be the weapons I'd use.

A thin, ferocious-looking woman stood behind those two beasts. She wore black combat armor and dark glasses. Her blond hair fell to her shoulders, framing her face. She crouched behind the door, keeping me in her sights.

"Drop them or I drop you," she commanded. Her slightly husky voice carried the intent that she hoped I disobeyed the order. "Do it. Now."

"You're making a—"

A crater appeared at my feet as she fired one of her guns. The deafening roar echoed into the night. Chunks of asphalt kicked up into my face.

"That was a courtesy," she warned. "Next hole appears in your chest."

I dropped the Twins. "I'm the—"

"Keep your hands where I can see them and get on your knees," she ordered. "Refuse or pause for more than three seconds and I blow your legs off to facilitate the kneeling. Your call."

I knelt down and kept my hands in the air.

They were a ragtag bunch on paper, but they seemed to be working pretty well as a team. I was guessing the one with the anger problem was Rose, my second-in-command. Made sense, considering she was obviously a hellion.

"Can I just—?" I started.

"Shut it," she snapped. "If I want to hear your voice, I'll ask a question. Did you hear me ask you anything?"

"No, it's just that I'm trying—"

She glared at me. "I said shut it," she snapped. "Has anyone seen the new chief? He should've been first on the scene."

The doors to the other cars started opening.

"Doe, Graffon, you two check the bar," Rose commanded, pointing to *The Dirty Goblin*, never taking her eyes off me. "Butch and Silk on the suspect. He so much as breathes the wrong way, put him down. I'm going to check what's left of the victims."

She made her way over to the crushed goblins and

crouched down touching the street. She examined the two goblins I shredded with Butterfly and glared at me again.

In front of me stood a dark fae sparkler, Silk Flitter, and what could only be described as a male in full valkyrie armor, definitely Butch. Their determined looks spelled that they were ready to stop me if I did anything besides breathe.

"Rose," said a voice from *The Dirty Goblin*, "you need to come see this."

Rose looked up and glanced at me again before heading to the bar.

"What is it, Graffon?" she said as she stepped through the window and peeked over the bar counter. Her face was dark as she immediately came back out out and approached me. "You have five seconds to explain why there's a dead hellion diplomat inside that bar."

"I've been trying to explain since you got here," I replied in an even voice.

I reached slowly in my jacket and all the guns pointed my way.

"You pull out anything besides ID and that's the last tug of your life."

"Phrasing," I mumbled.

"What?"

"Nothing."

I pulled out my ID and handed it to her.

"Well, shit." She said, as she read it and tossed it back to me. She looked over at the rest of the team. "Stand down."

"What about him?" Butch asked. "Isn't he dangerous?"

Everyone turned to face me.

I lowered my arms and stood, putting the wallet away.

"This"—Rose pointed at me with one of her guns—"is our new chief."

CHAPTER 4

"*J* guess the chief was the first one on the scene," Butch said.

"The chief *caused* the scene." Rose whirled on him with a snarl. "Are you not seeing this? What genius thought a dragon chief was a good idea?"

"Well, yes," Graffon, the demonoid, said as she pointed at the bodies, "but it seems like they all had relatively quick and painless deaths. And now *The Dirty Goblin* can renovate it's façade. That's an upside."

"Graffon? Shut up."

The demonoid didn't seem bothered by Rose's command. Voids, or faceless ones, were found on the fifth level of hell. That was the level of wrath. They were known for getting into your head, making you suffer through mental torment, depression, and downright lunacy. It was the rare individual who could make it past that level. Demons were essentially attorneys, though even scarier. They were tough, ruthless, powerful, and exacting. A demon would eat you just as soon as look at you, unless you were protected by a contract, or if they owed you one.

Graffon was a mixture of both.

A full-on void would have to wear a veil to protect others from falling into a pit of despair and self-loathing. Actually, Doe, the only full void on the team, was wearing a nice blue one with a rainbow unicorn painted on it. Don't ask; don't tell. Graffon, on the other hand, didn't appear to be affecting anyone negatively. So she was either able to flip that skill on at will or she didn't have the ability at all.

Percy came outside.

"You guys going to take the body?" he said, hooking an enormous thumb behind him. "I need to get ready for business."

"You've got no windows and half your bar is demolished, Percy," I noted, motioning toward the building.

He squinted. "So?"

"True," I acquiesced. Again, we *were* in the Badlands. Even in its current condition, *The Dirty Goblin* looked better than many bars further down the Strip. "Okay, guys, who handles taking away bodies here?"

"The Morgue," Graffon answered.

"You said that as if both words were capitalized."

"They are, Chief," she replied. "It's the biggest business in the Badlands. Employs more people than Badmart."

"Right." Obviously, I still had a lot to learn. "Well, get them down here so Percy can get back to business."

"What business?" Rose snapped, stepping close to me.

"Why didn't you call us earlier before this became a—whatever this is!"

"Clusterfuck?" I suggested.

Butch moaned and blushed. "Yes, please."

"Keep it in your pants," Rose warned, looking at the malkyrie for a few seconds. He held up his hands in surrender. She turned back to face me. "Your connector. Why didn't you call us?"

"I called Rowena—I mean Lady Rowena."

Silk giggled. "Did Nimble feed you the 'she thinks she's royalty' story?"

"I...uh..."

Damn it.

"If you're that gullible we're going to have a new chief inside a week," Rose groaned. Then, she shrugged. "Not that I see that as a bad thing necessarily."

"Pardon me?"

"Anyway," she continued, "we can all contact each other—*directly*. You don't need to go through Rowena."

"But Nimble told me—"

Rose stared at me and shook her head. "Where *did* they find you? Under a mountain?"

"Well, actually—"

"Don't care," she hissed.

Why did I feel like *she* was the real chief here?

"You do realize that you killing a hellion is going to cause an incident?"

"Wait a second here," I said holstering Pinky and Butterfly, "I didn't kill the guy. He came through the window dead." I gestured at the carnage in front of *The Dirty Goblin*. "Those goblins killed him."

Rose studied the area for a few moments, but she didn't seem to buy what I was selling.

"What do you mean you didn't kill him?" She scoffed, finally. "You're a dragon. Maybe the goblins were your henchmen, but I highly doubt you're an innocent party to this." Her hands were suddenly affixed to her hips. "That's like saying hellions aren't badass agents of death." She met my eyes. "We are."

The rest of the team nodded. I heard murmurs about dragons and rampages, of course. Someone said something about them being mindless killing machines. I guess 'them' was really 'us' considering I was one of them.

But enough was enough.

I was the boss here, not Rose.

"I didn't kill him," I stated evenly.

Rose looked around again.

"Well looks like all your witnesses are conveniently dead. Besides, who's going to vouch for a dragon?"

"I will," announced Percy. "Zeke's not lying. That hellion came through the window dead."

Rose walked up to Percy and had to look straight up to speak to him.

"So this is a frame up? That's what you're saying? Someone targeted your "—she spat to the side—"upscale establishment to frame the new chief?"

Percy put his hands on his hips. "I don't know what it is, lady," his voice thundered. "I'm just saying that the hellion was dead when he came through that window."

There was a moment of silence that I wished could have remained for hours. My brain was pounding like mad. I didn't know if that was from my partial change to dragon, my downing a full bottle of blood ale, or the fact that Percy had smacked me in the back of the head with a bottle, but it hurt like hell.

"These look like Company men," Silk noted. "Maybe they were trying to give the chief a funeral party?"

"Funeral party?" I asked confused. "What's that?"

"It's when The Company welcomes a new chief," Graffon answered. "The Company has full documentation and precedent for such matters. While I'm not exactly the contractual scholar that my father was—may his soul burn for all eternity—I know the basics." She began to pace.

"The very first thing The Company is required to do, based on their Articles of Incorporation, is to send out a welcome party to any new chief of the Badlands Paranormal Police Department. They usually do this by filling him with bullets." Her voice was oddly chipper. "Sometimes they use knives and axes. One time they used Molotov Cocktails, that party was hot."

"Stop trying to cheer him up, Graffon," Doe said. "The Company doesn't appreciate the PPD. Especially not the chief." His veil bounced a bit with each word, making the unicorn look as though it was dancing. "In case you haven't noticed."

"The bullets kind of gave it away," I acknowledged. "What's the bad blood about? Why don't they like the PPD?"

"We're cops," Rose said poking my chest. "They're criminals. They commit a crime and we dismember them and toss their body parts on the Strip, as a deterrent."

"Isn't that a little extreme?" I asked.

She pointed at the goblins I'd annihilated.

"Right."

"We don't actually dismember them, chief," Butch said, stepping close. "Right, Rose?"

"Speak for yourself," muttered Rose. "My method cuts recidivism to zero."

"We *arrest* and incarcerate the criminals, Rose," Butch stated. "Remember what the last chief said?"

Rose's shoulder dropped. "Yeah, yeah, yeah. 'The PPD is supposed to uphold the law, not be worse than the criminals'."

"Exactly," affirmed Butch.

"The last chief was right," I said quietly. "The PPD is meant to bring order to the Badlands."

They all stared at me.

"Wonderful," Rose said, rolling her eyes, "we've got a fucking honorable dragon leading us now. Graffon, you and Doe secure the perimeter. I'm going to go run preliminaries on the hellion before this shit storm gets out of control."

"So who's going to cover this damage?" Percy asked.

Rose glanced at Graffon. "All yours."

Graffon cleared her throat and Rose shook her head. "Prepare to have your brain melted."

"According to the clause in your insurance contract, the policy explicitly excludes and disclaims any and all losses and expenses of any nature whatsoever and however arising, but not limited to, direct, indirect, special, punitive, incidental and/or consequential damages including, but not limited to, loss of or damage to property or claims by third parties or other losses of any kind or character, even if the insurance company has been advised of the possibility of such damages or losses arising out of or caused and/or contributed to by agents or any agencies thereof or supernatural acts. Of course if you have a standard destruction clause in your insurance policy, that can affect other parts part of the coverage...

"Wait a second here," Percy called out. "If The Company is responsible for this, shouldn't they be forced to pay for the damages? Or...maybe *you* guys should. If it wasn't for the fact that you had a new chief, and if he hadn't shown up at my joint, this wouldn't have happened at all. Right?" He then winced at me. "Sorry, Zeke, but I gotta pay for this somehow."

Rose snapped her fingers at Graffon, pointed at Percy, and then pulled me away. I glanced over my shoulder to see Graffon stepping up to handle Percy's complaint.

"By the time she's done with him," Rose explained, "she'll have him pay for the damages and offer to sell her *The Dirty Goblin* at a discount in order to pay us for any psychological distress he may have caused." Rose looked back at Graffon. "Don't mess with demons."

"This is Leon's territory." Silk noted, as we headed toward the PPD cars. "I'll take Butch and see what we can dig up."

They were all nodding as Rose dragged me back toward Percy and Graffon.

She was seriously strong and supremely confident, but pretty soon I was going to have to exert control over this situation. For now, though, I would let it play out a little longer. There was no point in me puffing my chest out when I was clearly the least knowledgable person on the force at the moment.

Graffon was wrapping up her legal diatribe when we returned.

"...and, therefore," she said to the glassy-eyed Percy, "you will cease and desist all discussions related, but not limited to, the potentiality of litigation against the Badlands Paranormal Police Department, its officers, its chief, or any of its assigns. Are we clear?"

Percy swallowed hard and nodded harder.

"So," I ventured, "who is Leon again?"

"Leon is a lieutenant for Rake Masters," Percy answered quickly, pulling his eyes away from Graffon. He then nearly sprinted back into *The Dirty Goblin*. We followed. "Masters is the head of The Company," Percy continued. "He controls it. If these are Leon's thugs, The Company is definitely sending you a message."

"Yeah," Rose laughed in a not-so-funny way. "The message is 'get gone or get dead'. Standard new chief stuff."

I stared down at the fallen hellion.

"This your first body?" Rose asked, dropping down and searching the pockets of the guy.

She looked at the ID Zeke handed her and grimaced.

"As a cop, yes," I said.

"Well, look at you," she said, giving me a golf clap. "Caught a body on day one. I'll have a plaque made up." She stopped clapping and got serious. "Before I investigate further, you're *sure* you didn't dust this hellion?"

"Positive," I said. "Think I'd remember killing a

hellion."

"Can't really tell with dragons," she grunted, showing me the ID. "He's from House Malevolent. This just went from shit storm to shit tsunami."

"Aren't those two the same—?"

"House Mal isn't going to bother with pleasantries," she interrupted. "Once they find out" —she looked at the ID again—"Henry here is dead, they're going to want the perp. One guess which dragon is going to be on the top of *that* list?"

"I didn't kill him."

"*Nimble,*" Rose's voice said through the connector, indicating I'd been included on the group call, "*run a cross reference on a diplomat hellion, one Henry Malevolent. I need to know why he was in town. Business? Pleasure? A little of both? Also, I need known associates.*"

"*How's the new chief?*" Nimble asked. "*Still alive?*"

"*Yep. You owe me fifty.*"

"*Shit.*" Nimble grumbled. "*Uh...no offense, chief. It just that we had a deadpool.*"

"*Some taken,*" I replied.

"*Uh...I'll have the info for you in two hours, Rose. Unless you need it sooner?*"

"*Within my lifetime would be great.*"

"*Then you should have called me earlier.*"

"Slugs," Rose said, shaking her head. "While he's dragging his feet, let's see what we can find out."

I held up a finger. "Just how bad *is* House Malevolent?"

Rose gave a short laugh and nodded out the window.

"Let's just say that you're going to wish those goblins had had better aim."

CHAPTER 5

*W*e stepped over to the mangled mess of vehicles. Rose bent down and touched the ground.

She raised her fingers to her nose and sniffed.

Then, she walked over to the car I'd shoved before earlier that evening.

It looked less like a car and more like abstract art. The goblin bodies were still crushed on the other side.

Rose leaned over and examined them.

"You did this?" she asked, looking at the damage. "I don't see entry wounds." She raised an eyebrow. "You just crushed them?"

I nodded. "They were making an effort to fill me with bullets."

"How did you do it?" she questioned, standing up and putting her hands on her hips. "Show me."

I placed a foot on one of the cars and pushed. The car slid effortlessly across the street.

Rose nodded and stepped close. "The fact that you can

do that without breaking a sweat only makes you look bad," she warned. "Don't go showing off that strength until we find out who did this. Got it?"

"And if I need to use it?" I asked, as she stepped back to *The Dirty Goblin*. I needed to shift the perception of power. I *was* the Chief, after all. "I don't intend to let anyone use me for target practice."

"Listen, I know you're new," Rose said. "Frankly, I don't care how you got this position. What I do know is that some wet behind the ears dragon isn't going to jeopardize this team."

"I wasn't planning on—" I started.

"Get up to speed or get dead." She shot back under her breath. "If you feel the need to show off your strength, you'd better understand the consequences that come with that."

"What are you talking about?" I said, glancing around. "What consequences?"

"What do you see over there?"

"You mean Graffon and Doe?"

"Targets," Rose said, looking away. "Every member of the Badlands PPD is a target for every little piece of scum that crawls through this hellhole."

"Shit," I said, realizing how covering my ass meant widening the target on my new team. "I didn't mean—"

"Do I look like I give a flying fu..." She took a slow breath and exhaled. "I don't care what you meant. Meanings and feelings will get you killed out here."

Things grew quiet for a second. At least between us. Percy was still moaning and groaning as he did his best to sweep up the glass and put his tables back in order. I had the feeling that it was going to take a lot more than a broom and some brawn to fix the damage.

That was sad, really. Percy seemed like a decent guy, even for a troll...*especially* for a troll. Not that I knew a lot of trolls or anything, but those I'd run into during my training stints with the valkyries weren't exactly what you'd consider cuddly. Most of them only smiled when they were cutting a swath of destruction. They loved taking people and smashing them together to make sculptures. Some of their creations were oddly amazing. Morbid, but incredible. I couldn't help but think that if they'd had a decent-sized set of Legos in their formative years, they wouldn't be so mentally deranged as adults.

"Are you even from the Badlands?" Rose asked in a condescending way.

"Yes," I said, managing to keep my anger in check. I couldn't afford to let my anger get away from me and go dragon. "I was raised by valkyries."

She stared at me. "If that's your attempt at humor, I think I'd rather stare into Doe's face."

I gave her a harsh look. Deliberately staring into the face of a void was to die a horrible death. Of course, that depended on how strong you were. Some people could have a lengthy conversation with a void and it wouldn't affect them in the least. Others, though, got depressed incredibly fast and usually ended up doing themselves in or going out and doing something very naughty to others.

"That's not funny."

"Neither are you," she answered. "Now I'm going to assume that you didn't just get this position because you're connected."

"I trained with—"

"DGAF." Rose held up a finger. "Before The Morgue or an emissary from House Malevolent gets here, review the scene and tell me what you see."

I furrowed my brow at her.

"Donkey Goat Ape Foragers?"

"What?"

"Yeah, that last one doesn't make much sense," I replied, rubbing my chin. "Can't think of an animal that starts with F..." I snapped my finger. "Fox! Is it fox?"

It was her turn to do the brow furrowing.

"What the hell are you talking about?"

"DGAF."

"Don't Give A Fuck," she deadpanned.

"Oh, I see," I said, with a roll of my eyes. "I'm the new guy, so I don't get to know what all the cool acronyms mean yet."

"That *is* what it means."

I blinked. Then, I played the letters over again.

"Ohhh. Right." I coughed. "Sorry."

Then, I looked over the destruction and carnage. As a dragon, my senses were heightened beyond other supernaturals, except maybe hellions. I stepped over to the totaled cars, avoiding the still smoldering truck. In the rear seat of one of the vehicles, I smelled blood.

I leaned inside the car and sniffed around.

"Hellion blood mixed with goblin blood," I stated.

"What does that—"

I held up a finger and tried to build a picture of what I imagined had happened in here.

"There were two goblins, one on each side. The hellion

was in the middle." I zoomed my vision on the seat. "His hands were being held down at his sides." I continued my scan. "They killed him back here but not before he fought back and drew blood. It took three of them to kill him. Two to hold him at bay...mostly...and the one from the front seat to stab him."

Rose nodded. "Seems Henry wasn't going down without a fight. What else?" She held up her wrist. "Tick tock, Columbo."

I looked at the position of the cars in relation to *The Dirty Goblin* window. I walked the distance from the car with the goblin blood to the shattered storefront.

"Rose," Graffon called out, "we've got The Morgue incoming."

I looked down the street and saw a black truck with a large golden M printed on the sides. They were approaching slowly.

"Keep them outside the perimeter until I say so," Rose replied and turned to me. "Don't overthink it. It's usually the thing that's staring you in the face."

We stood in front of the bar and I looked at the cars again. "How strong is a goblin?"

"Good question, keep on."

I walked back to the car and turned to *The Dirty Goblin*. "That's about forty feet. How much do you weigh? Hellions are pretty dense."

"Are you calling me fat?" Rose narrowed her eyes at me and let one of her hands rest on one of her guns. "Have you grown tired of breathing?"

"Get over yourself," I shot back as I stepped over to dead Henry. "He's about your size," I said, and then pointed at *The Dirty Goblin*'s façade. "He sailed through the window at force, smashing into and over the bar."

I crouched down to examine the small crater Henry's head had left in the dense wood. None of the bullets had penetrated the bar.

"Percy," I said, rubbing a finger over some of the bullet depressions in the wood, "what kind of wood is this?" It felt really strange. "This is wood, right?"

Percy nodded, crossing his massive arms over his chest

"Why is that even releva—?" Rose started.

I gave her a sharp look, tiring of this little power play. I was the chief here, not Rose.

"Is your name Percy now?" I asked her with an edge.

"Excuse me," she replied with wide eyes.

"You're excused," I said. "Now, if you'll let Percy answer my question, we can get on with things." I held up my wrist at her. "Tick tock, remember?"

To her credit, she didn't kill me.

"Troll Buloke," Percy answered. "We call it ironwood."

"Ironwood," Rose said, her face immediately on the mend. Apparently, she was impressed with Percy's admission. "That stuff is denser than steel and ten times as expensive."

"I believe in being prepared," Percy said, looking at Rose. "This isn't my first bar and I don't enjoy bullet holes."

"How did you afford a piece of ironwood this large?" she questioned.

"I know a troll who knows a guy," Percy replied, his voice going cold.

Rose shook her head and looked at me. "Wrap it up or

The Morgue is going to run over Doe and Graffon to get to the bodies."

"Goblins aren't strong enough to throw a hellion forty feet fast enough to shatter the window and put a dent in ironwood," I said, ignoring her. "And none of the windshields were destroyed, so he wasn't launched through the vehicle."

Rose tilted her head. "What are you saying?"

"The only species I know that's strong enough to throw a hellion that far and that fast is—" Rose and I both turned to face Percy—"a troll."

CHAPTER 6

"*D*ragons are just as strong, if not stronger when they turn," Percy said. "Besides, I was in here with you."

"True," I answered. "I was so focused on the paperwork I didn't notice if there was anyone else besides Leon's thugs."

"*Black limo headed your way,*" Graffon's voice came over the group channel. "*Doe didn't feel like getting run over to stop it, even when I explained how easily multiple fractures can heal.*"

"*No thanks,*" Doe said. "*Broken everything doesn't sound remotely fun.*"

"*Who is it?*" Rose asked. "*Can you tell from the markings?*"

"*Some bigshot from House Malevolent—get ready for incoming.*"

"Shit," Rose said under her breath. "Let me do the talking."

"No," I said. She and Percy both turned to look at me.

Percy gave me a 'expect a smackdown' smile and Rose scowled. "I got this."

"You got this?" she asked, incredulously. "You have no idea what you *got*."

Again, I needed to assert my position. Rose was second-in-command, but I was the chief. She may have experience dealing with people as a cop, and I'd definitely have to lean on that experience over time, but I knew how these things went. If I didn't grab the reins fast, I'd be an impotent leader.

"I'm the chief, Rose," I stated coolly, after pulling her away from Percy so we could speak in private. "That means I deal with diplomatic matters of importance involving the Badlands and the Houses. I know I'm new to all this, and I'm definitely going to want your input, but I was never one to use training wheels."

Rose raised her hands in surrender and backed up.

"Your funeral," she said, turning to the bar. "You have any blood ale left, troll?"

"The name is Percy."

"Yeah, whatever," Rose snapped back. "Pour a glass of homebrewed. It better not be that commercial piss or I'll shoot you myself."

Percy nodded as if this was standard fair for how his customers treated him. Then, he removed one of the few intact glasses and handed her a bottle.

"Homebrewed, pure," he said, almost proudly. "Guaranteed to light your ass on fire. Even an ass as fine as yours."

"We'll see," Rose said, grabbing the glass and bottle. I was surprised she didn't backhand him for the comment on her derrière. "You'd better get ready, just in case our chief starts a diplomatic 'incident' with House Mal."

That didn't exactly give me a boost of confidence.

I took a deep breath and stepped outside to greet the approaching limo. Behind it was another truck similar to The Morgue vehicle. This one was missing the large M on the sides, though.

The limo itself was a sleek affair with what I could only guess was the crest of House Malevolent on the doors.

It pulled up short of the wreckage and stopped.

The driver's door opened and a formally dressed hellion stepped out, and opened the rear passenger door. A tall, suited hellion stepped out disregarding the driver. His clothing screamed excess. This wasn't some low-level functionary. Going by the attitude and limo, this was an important dude.

"Oh shit," Rose said, obviously having followed me out, bottle and all. "They sent Emissary Sinclair."

"Who is Emissary Sinclair?" I asked. "And what position does he hold in House Mal?"

"Nope," Rose said, pulling the cork out of the bottle with her teeth with one swift tug and spitting it across the street. She poured blood ale into her glass, leaned against one of the wrecked Company vehicles, and then raised the drink in my direction. "You got this. Unleash the diplomatic skills your species is known for."

She waved me on with her hand.

"Bitch," I said.

"Next time don't utilize the group channel to compliment me," Rose's voice came over the channel. *"Damn noobs."*

"Fuck me," I muttered under my breath as the hellion emissary stood next to the limo, examining his fingers.

Clearly, he was waiting for me.

"No one is going to take you up on that. Remember, you got this, Chief."

Okay, so it was obvious that I hadn't yet mastered the connector.

I crossed over to Emissary Sinclair and extended my hand.

"Zeke Phoenix, Chief of the Badlands PPD." He glanced down at my outstretched hand and raised an eyebrow.

I dropped my hand and felt my eye begin to twitch.

Looking over his shoulder, Sinclair gave a nod and the other morgue-like truck drove close.

"You're a...dragon?" Sinclair asked.

I nodded.

"We have the crime scene secure and we will—"

The Morgue-like truck Sinclair had summoned drove to the front of *The Dirty Goblin.*

"I'm here for the body." Sinclair gazed at me. "I trust the perpetrator of this heinous act will be apprehended?"

"We're working on it at the moment. Do you know why your diplomat would be—?"

"Very well, Mr. Kleenex," Sinclair interrupted. "I'm sure your PPD people are hard at work, doing whatever it is you do."

"It's Phoenix, and I'm going to need you to call your people out of my crime scene."

"Excuse me, *dragon?*" Sinclair sneered. "Do you know who you are addressing?"

"The next inmate of my jail if you don't remove your people from my crime scene."

"How dare you?"

I turned to look at Rose.

"Can you believe this guy?"

She furrowed her brow at me for a moment, but a slow smile crept onto her face.

"You're playing him?" she said in a direct-connection. *"That's your strategy?"*

"Can you think of a better one?" I replied.

"This should prove interesting."

"I'm glad you think so because I'm about to turn him over to you. Don't go out of your way to be nice, either."

Her smile grew even wider.

"Upperclass wonk," she said aloud. "Being a douche is second nature to him. Can't help it."

"I…" The guy nearly shrieked. "What did you just call me, you loathsome peon?"

"I see what you mean, Rose," I stated with a nod. "Does seem like an uppity shit."

"I'll have you know that I can single-handedly—"

"Pal," I interrupted with a wince, "I have *zero* desire to know the things you do with yourself 'single-handedly'."

Rose snorted and began to cough.

"The nerve," breathed Sinclair, his face a priceless visage of shock and anger.

"You'd better talk to this hellion before I have him physically removed from this active crime scene," I said, spinning back to my second-in-command.

Rose nodded and tossed the empty bottle of blood ale behind her.

"Chief says you need to vacate the premises," Rose lowered her voice. "You vacate the premises."

"A diplomat was killed, which makes this a House matter," Sinclair countered, taking a step back from Rose. "Local law enforcement has no jurisdiction—"

"Graffon," I called out, "can you explain to this pompous suppository precisely how jurisdiction works in the Badlands?"

"That's Emissary, you...*dragon*," Sinclair spat.

"Imagine how offended I am to be called a dragon," I deadpanned.

He swallowed and looked around. "It was meant to sound derisive."

"Guess you need a little practice, then, Sinclair." Then, I held up my hand. "I'm sorry, I meant *Emissary Sinclair*."

I'd said his full title with as much derision as I could muster.

Graffon approached and began explaining jurisdictional statutes. While Sinclair was definitely a complete asshat, I couldn't help but feel bad about the fact that Graffon was going to saddle him with the mother of all headaches.

I headed back to *The Dirty Goblin* with Rose in tow.

"Nicely done, Chief," she said in a voice of awe. "It's not often that someone rattles a hellion, and on day one, too." I didn't know how fast blood ale worked on hellions, but her attitude swap could have just been a case of her being a wee bit tipsy. "Maybe there's hope for you yet."

"Thanks," I replied. "I hope I didn't cause an incident."

"You probably did," Rose said, glancing over at Graffon

and the cornered Sinclair. "He'll cry to his superiors who'll send a real threat."

We paused and looked around the scene again.

"You're either the smartest chief I've ever seen, or the dumbest," Rose added. "It's only your first day and you've just made a couple of great enemies. I call that going above and beyond."

"Thanks, I think." Then, I looked at her. "A couple of great enemies?"

"Well, you already have The Company after you."

"Fair enough," I acquiesced, "but that's just because I'm the new chief, right?"

She nodded. "That's how it started, yeah, but then you went and killed a bunch of goblins and destroyed their cars."

"Oh, right." I glanced back outside and watched as workers from The Morgue loaded the charred remains of a goblin into the hearse. "At least I haven't pissed off anyone else yet."

"The day's still young, Chief," Rose snarked. "At the rate you're going, your replacement will be in place before the end of our shift."

"That'd be you, right?" I asked, giving her a look.

She smirked and gave me a slight shrug.

"Before you start getting too ambitious, Rose," I pointed out, "you may want to take a good look around and see what it is you'll be inheriting."

Her face fell.

"Shit," she mumbled.

"Yep."

CHAPTER 7

The Morgue personnel carted away what was left of the goblins and Henry, the hellion diplomat. Sinclair fumed and threatened to have me fired. I thought he meant getting me kicked off the PPD. He meant really fired—tied to a steel stake and set ablaze until my bones turned to ash.

It's hard to kill a dragon with fire, but I was still quite hurtable...especially out of dragon form. I don't know if I could burn to death, though, and I sure as shit wasn't eager to find out.

"How did House Mal find out about Henry so fast?" I asked Rose, as we jumped into her Hurricane.

She drove.

"The better question is who killed the hellion and why?" Rose said, turning her car around and speeding down the street.

"Both good questions." I held onto the handle near the door. "Are we in a hurry?"

To say Rose drove fast would be like saying Percy was a little on the large side.

The Hurricane's sleek frame seemed to sink into the ground as she accelerated. Her driving wasn't so much swerving through traffic as discovering how close she could get without colliding before switching lanes. I sensed another Chief hazing moment and kept my cool.

Rose glanced over and grinned, clearly enjoying my discomfort.

"Your car is back at the precinct," she said. "You'll be able to drive on your own next time."

"Good," I replied, thinking I'd be safer if I partially transformed into dragon about now. "Anyway, you were saying about the hellion?"

"House Mal will send someone to The Morgue, especially after you blocked Sinclair." Rose answered, as she cut over two lanes and deftly inserted the Hurricane between two cars, before sliding out and flooring the gas pedal while shifting into high gear. "We need to get there before they do."

"I applaud your work ethic," I said holding my breath as she nearly rammed a truck. "You think we could work it so we get there in one piece and not part of a totaled PPD vehicle?"

"Are you questioning my driving ability?" she asked, cutting off another car.

"Driving? Is that what you're calling it?"

"I was top of my class in the PPD Defensive Driving course."

"Was there a course left when you were done?"

I winced as she grazed the side of another vehicle. We

were so close I could reach out and touch the driver if we weren't approaching Mach 1.

"Yes, mostly." She smiled at the memory. "Driving is my thing. Do not question my driving." She gave me a quick look and smirked. "By the way, your scales are showing."

I pulled them back in.

"I thought your thing was being a badass agent of death, Rose?"

She glanced over again and held my gaze for longer than I thought necessary while dodging traffic to make her point.

"My driving falls under the 'badass' umbrella. Now, shut it while I check the status of the bodies."

"More like reckless endangerment," I muttered, as she caused a few more cars to swerve behind us.

"Rowena, give me a status on The Morgue truck."

I heard Rose's voice through my connector.

"Hello, Rose," Rowena answered. *"The Morgue vehicle is currently in transit and barring any unforeseen events, should arrive at The Morgue in twenty minutes."*

"Unforeseen events?" I asked. *"What do you mean?"*

"Oh, you're still alive," Rowena answered icily. *"And you still haven't learned how to properly address your superiors."*

Rose smiled and covered it with a short cough. *"Ro, keep me posted and send me an alert the moment they pull in."*

"Of course."

"You get to call her 'Ro' and 'Rowena'? I asked. "How come she doesn't give you the whole 'Lady Rowena' treatment?"

"Might have something to do with a conversation I

had with Nimble," Rose glanced in the rear-view mirror and then at me. "Tighten your harness."

"I'm going to have to speak to Nimble," I said. "Last thing I need is an AI giving me attitude...wait what?"

"Someone really has a hard-on for you, Chief."

Rose sped up, swerved left and down shifted, avoiding a speeding vehicle. It was a sleek black item and sped off before I could get a good look at the driver. She changed lanes as another car sideswiped us into the center median.

"Who the hell was—?" I started as I turned just in time to see the truck smash the rear of the Hurricane, launching us into the air.

CHAPTER 8

*T*he Hurricane tumbled slowly through the air. In one smooth motion, Rose undid her seat harness, kicked open the driver's side door, and braced herself, looking over at me.

"You plan on staying?" she asked. "I can guarantee you these vehicles aren't meant for flight."

The fact that she could say that with such certainty was disturbing.

I glanced quickly out the window. "We're airborne."

"Not for long, Captain Obvious," she snarked, drawing both her guns and jumping. "Meet you on the ground."

I opened my door and the rush of air hit me in the face. It was clear hellions were insane, but she was right. If I stayed in the car it didn't matter how tough dragons were, I was in for a world of pain. I looked down and leapt into the air, realizing this was a horrible idea as the Hurricane tumbled away from me.

I didn't know if this latest attack was still part of the funeral party or not.

What I *did* know was that I needed to make a statement.

I unleashed some of the pent up rage from being the target of repeated attacks. My skin transformed back to scales. Below, I noticed Rose firing at the truck that tried to turn us into roadkill.

It was time to pull out Pinky.

One of the things I enjoyed about shotguns, precision aiming was a suggested skill, not a prerequisite. This was especially true with Pinky and the dragon rounds. I fired at the truck as the road reached up to greet me like a giant fist. Then, I grunted in pain, rolling for several feet, protected by my scales.

A wall of flame raced down the street following the roar of the explosion. Vehicles veered off the road and onto the sidewalks and other vehicles. I looked ahead as Rose walked over.

"I did want to ask them some questions," she said holstering her guns. "Might be a little difficult now. Looks like your scales are back."

The truck was a burnt out husk. I looked down at Pinky. I knew the dragon rounds packed a punch, but they were never this strong.

I got my anger under control and the scales faded from sight.

After holstering my shotgun, I walked over to the truck. The smell of accelerant was quite noticeable.

"These guys weren't supposed to kick us into the air," I said moving to the front of what was left of the truck. I knew what I would find there. "They were supposed to explode on contact. Your driving saved us from an instant barbecue."

"Badass," she said pointing to herself. "Let me guess? The cab is empty?"

I nodded.

"This thing was just one big bomb." I looked around the Strip. "This is my first day. I haven't been on the job long enough to make these kinds of enemies. You sure someone isn't trying to retire *you*?"

"I'm not the chief," Rose replied, crossing her arms. "Besides, my enemies are the 'stand close and shove a blade into your heart' type."

"Nice," I said, as we walked over to the flipped Hurricane. "You're saying this is part of that funeral party?"

"Give me a hand," Rose instructed, as she reached under the Hurricane. "Could be, or it could be a warm welcome from someone else. PPD Chiefs are popular in the Badlands—as victims."

"That's a refreshing thought," I crouched down next to her.

On her signal, we lifted and flipped the car over. It was a fair bit lighter than I'd expected, and I'd be lying if I said I'd done the lion's share of the lifting. Rose was seriously strong. That was a common trait for hellions, but they weren't typically as strong as dragons.

One more thing to keep my eye on.

The world of the Badlands PPD was ever rotating. Chief today, dead tomorrow. That's how it rolled out. Other levels of cops got killed too, of course, but they weren't usually targeted. If anything, they died because they were in the wrong place at the wrong time. Namely, standing too close to the chief when the bullets started flying. But it was also well known that the position of chief was filled by the highest-ranking person next in rotation. Seeing that the hellions followed hell, that put Rose in line for the job next.

Something told me she wasn't exactly itching for the position, though. It probably had to do with how many times she'd pointed out that I would soon be dead due to the fact that I was the new chief. Basic logic would have to dictate that she'd fall to the same fate within days of my demise, should she actually land the position.

Still, I was planning to keep one eye on her. If the valkyries taught me anything, it was that people craved power. If history taught the world anything, it was that hellions craved it more than anyone…including dragons.

I shook my head, surprised to find the car didn't have a scratch on it.

"You sure this thing still works?"

"This Hurricane Interceptor is the hellion of PPD vehicles. My baby is as tough as I am." Rose patted the top of the vehicle. "Let's go secure The Morgue. After that, we need to pay Windham a visit."

"Windham?" I asked, not recognizing the name as we jumped into the car. Rose started the engine with a roar. "He's not in any of my notes."

"He wouldn't be," Rose turned onto the Strip and sped forward, "but he's the only person who would know where the accelerant you smelled came from."

"What is he?" I asked, while working to attach my seatbelt. "Some kind of chemist?"

"Something like that," she answered, turning off the Strip and heading down a broad boulevard. "He does property reclamation work for The Company."

"He's in construction?"

"More like deconstruction. Windham is an explosives expert."

CHAPTER 9

"*A*re you saying this Windham devised the truck bomb?" I asked, as we pulled up to the rear of The Morgue.

It was a squat, brown, windowless building. It had more in common with a fort than what I imagined The Morgue would look like.

Rose shook her head. "If Wind had made the truck bomb, we'd be picking up little dragon bits right about now."

I noticed how she omitted her demise from the explosion. "Really, hellions are bombproof?"

"Hellions are stupid-proof," Rose answered. "We don't go around firing explosive rounds at trucks filled *with* explosives and covered in accelerant. You were the one who smelled the accelerant, right?"

"Not while I was flying through the air," I countered. "I was focused on not landing on my face."

"Might've been an improvement. Anyway, you should

have sensed the contents well ahead of time. You're a dragon, remember?"

She was right. I allowed the situation to overwhelm my senses. If I was going to be chief, I needed to remain calm in these kinds of scenarios. The valkyries would have been shaking their heads at me right about now.

"I saw you shooting at it, too," I said, though a bit more subdued, "so maybe we're both sharing a bit in the shoot-first-think-later pool."

"I was shooting at the tires." She shook her head and got out of the car. "*You* were being a typical dragon. Raze everything to the ground and sift through the ash later. That won't work out here."

It was clear that she had no idea about my background. I may have been many things, but a typical dragon was not one of them. At least, I assumed I wasn't, considering I hadn't lived among dragons for over twenty years.

The last time I was with my own kind, there had been some sort of accident. I was fourteen, had just reached the age of ascension, and during my maiden flight in full dragon, there had been a collision.

The dragons who were with me had assumed I was dead. When I awoke, I was surrounded by valkyries. They'd explained everything that had happened. It left a bitter taste in my mouth to know that my fellow dragons had just left me there to rot. So, I followed suit, marking the dragons as dead in my world.

The valkyries became my new family. I learned their ways as best I could, which meant that I wasn't acting as much like a dragon as I was acting as a valkyrie...or maybe an odd combination of both.

I just saw no point in arguing about it at the moment.

"This is The Morgue?" I said, looking around the area, unimpressed. "Am I to guess that they ran out of funding?"

"This" —she pointed to the squat structure in front of us—"is the entrance to The Morgue. You see those units?"

She swept an arm to the side. I followed the motion and saw the squat refrigeration units. They covered the area to either side of the entrance for what seemed like a mile or more.

"Those are part of—?" I began, taking in the scope.

"Most of The Morgue is underground," she replied, climbing the stairs to the entrance. "After we had that *incident*, it was safer to keep the bodies several levels below the surface."

"Safer for whom?" I asked entering the building next to her.

"Good question," she flashed her ID to the heavily armed guards at the door. "I'd like to say safer for us."

I followed her example and showed the guards my ID. They took a few moments longer comparing the picture to my face. After a few double checks, the guard silently waved us through.

"What was that about?" I asked, as we headed to the stairs. "He's never seen a dragon?"

"I'm sure he's seen plenty. He was probably just surprised to see that the new chief was still alive."

"Nice." I grunted. "And since when does a morgue need heavily armed guards?"

She glanced at me.

"Are you sure you're from the Badlands?" she asked. "Creatures get out of The Morgue enough times to make it dangerous. Things that are supposed to be dead don't stay dead, or they start out dead and then get less dead. Complete pain in the ass."

We reached the lowest level and another guard checkpoint.

Rose nodded at one of the guards. They returned the bro-nod and waved us through. I couldn't see their faces due to the helmets that connected to their body armor. Rose stopped in the corridor after the checkpoint and pointed at the guard with the name tag that read 'Allen.'

"House Mal is sending some representatives to *reclaim* a body. No one gets down here without PPD authorization. Understood?" she commanded, looking at Allen.

"Yes, ma'am," one of the guards next to Allen answered. Allen elbowed him in the ribs. "Quiet."

Rose stepped over to the guard who answered. His name was Davies.

"Next time you 'ma'am' me, you sniveling little ass pimple, I'm going to rip your legs off. We clear?"

Davies nodded vigorously and tried to step back.

"I got this," Allen explained to Rose. "Sorry, he's new."

"If he doesn't want to become a permanent resident, teach him how to address the PPD." Rose spun and began walking down the corridor. "Next time I won't be so cordial. And remember, *no one* comes down here."

"Got it," Allen called back. "We won't let anyone through."

We passed several large doorways and came to one at the end of the corridor.

"This is us," Rose said as she stopped in front of the door. "Get ready."

She pushed it open and stepped inside.

"What would I need to get ready for?" I answered. "It's a morgue, remember?"

I stepped through.

I wasn't ready.

CHAPTER 10

I'd never been inside a morgue before, but I had a feeling this was far from the norm.

The first thing I noticed was the cold. Dragons aren't exactly built for sub-zero temperatures. It didn't stop me in this form, but I was aware the environment would affect some of my abilities in this underground facility.

Long corridors ran off to either side of us. Each one was made up of long modular mortuary coolers in a stacked configuration. Some of them were thin, others were abnormally large. A long, narrow, metal staircase covered in frost led up to a platform several feet above us.

Rose climbed the stairs two at a time.

When we reached the top, we were greeted with a top down view of The Morgue. More armed guards dressed like the two we met earlier patrolled the labyrinth of corridors beneath us.

"How large is this place?" I asked, looking around from our bird's-eye view.

"I haven't measured it, but I know this is the largest

morgue in the Netherworld." Rose said, glancing over the edge of the railing. "And it goes down several more levels."

"This place is immense." I could see there were several levels below us. "How many people man this place?"

"A small army of assorted creatures handle the running of The Morgue," Rose answered, "but it's managed by Francis and Fitz."

"Francis and Fitz?" I asked. "Who are Francis and Fitz?"

"We don't really know *what* Francis is…some of us think he's a hybrid of some kind and we don't talk about Fitz. But listen, when you see Fitz, do *not* stare."

"Why would I stare?"

"Everyone stares. Just try to be subtle about it. Fitz doesn't like it. The last thing I need or want is to deal with an angry Fitzroy."

"His actual name is Fitzroy…seriously?"

"Really?" she said with a sigh. "You're going to point out names, when you're running around the Badlands with a moniker like Zeke?"

She had a point.

"Touché."

"Remember, don't stare."

"I won't, I promise," I answered, after Rose fixed me with an icy glare. "I'd be more interested in knowing the actual size of this place. How could the PPD not know the—"

"The actual size of The Morgue is classified information," a voice said from behind us. "We keep that information hidden to prevent a cataclysmic event…like war."

I turned and faced the smallish figure dressed in a white lab coat. His hair was a disheveled orange explosion covering piercing green eyes, which stared at us from behind a pair of thick-rimmed glasses. A pocket protector peeked out from the lab coat holding an assortment of pens and instruments. As odd as the small man looked, I wasn't prepared for the lumbering figure shuffling close behind him. He—at least I think it was a he —stood as tall as tall as a troll but that wasn't what threw me.

This *creature,* which, every passing second confirmed was the only way to describe what I was looking at, had the body of a troll, the head of a goblin and, judging from the markings, the arms of a Valkyrie.

I stared.

"Francis," Rose said, turning and elbowing me in the ribs with dark eyes, "what's cooking?"

"Rose," Francis answered, revealing a smile of pointed teeth. "It's good to see you. Are you the one keeping me busy today?"

Rose pointed at me with her chin. "He's the one who sent you the goblins."

"And the hellion?" Francis turned to face me and gave me a once over. It felt oddly like being sized up for an examination table. "Was that his handiwork as well?"

"That's what we're here to find out." Rose narrowed her eyes at me again.

Clearly, I was still staring.

"Can you tell us anything?" asked Francis.

"Uh...yeah," I said, shaking myself. "The hellion was dead by the time he arrived at *The Dirty Goblin.* Or, if he wasn't, he was dead the second his head was introduced to that ironwood bar at speed. I didn't kill him."

"So you must be the new chief?" Francis held out a hand. "Surprising to see you, still alive that is."

"Zeke," I said, taking the hand and squeezing. I usually had to be careful in these situations and not use too much of my dragon strength. I didn't know what Francis was, but his strength was easily on par with mine as he shook my hand with an iron grip. "Zeke Phoenix."

"Sounds like a superhero name," Francis noted. "Have you a cape hidden somewhere?"

"No," I replied, furrowing my brow.

"Right. Well, I'm Francis Nimrod Stein. You can call me Frank Or Francis."

"Your name is Frank N. Stein?" I asked, glancing briefly at Fitz. "Are you serious?"

Francis stared at me for a few seconds. "I was under the impression dragons possessed acute senses of hearing, and I don't believe I mumbled."

"No, I heard you. It's just...never mind."

"I told Mary to insist on Modern Prometheus and keep my name out of it," Francis said with a small shake of his head. "Did she listen?"

"I'm going to say no?"

"Exactly," Francis replied with a sigh. "She didn't listen and I still get comments. I should have never encouraged her."

Wait, was he talking about Mary Shelley here?

"*You* encouraged her?" I was baffled, blinking at him repeatedly. "Are you saying that *you* are the impetus behind Frankenstein?"

"Of course," he replied. "Did you think she came up with that story on her own?"

"Well, yes?"

Francis stared at me, looked at Rose, and returned his gaze to me.

"Were you raised in the Badlands?"

"Actually—" I started.

"Not important," Francis interrupted with a wave of his hand. "In any case, you wouldn't believe the comments I get at the annual Mortuary Administrators and Director Scientists Conference every year."

"How bad can it be?" I asked. "I mean you deal with dead—"

"The mostly dead—in addition to the maintenance on my assistant."

"That would explain the guards," I muttered under my breath.

"Indeed." Francis led the way down the staircase closest to us. "The questions are incessant, and often the same ones. Does your assistant ever lose himself in The Morgue? Francis, how does he keep it together at The Morgue? Does the work ever get so bad your assistant falls to pieces?"

"Must be annoying," I said, trying to keep a straight face. "Sounds like they may be a bit jealous."

"Of course they're jealous," Francis answered. "None of them have been able to create life!"

I glanced at Fitz, giving him a once over. As far as creating life went, he was hanging on by a fingernail and it was at risk of being yanked out.

"Create life?" I asked. "You sure he doesn't qualify as the mostly dead?"

"Mistake," Rose said as she shook her head.

Francis whirled on me when we reached the bottom of the stairs. "I'm sorry. Are you a medical professional?"

"I'm not really—"

"Have you taken the dead flesh of several corpses and sewn it together?"

"Not really my expertise. I'm more—"

"Have you harnessed the power of creation and reanimated said dead flesh?" Francis continued, raising his voice. "Have you brought life to what was once rotting and decaying matter?"

"Can't say that I have," I answered.

"Precisely! Only *I* have achieved this feat. I alone, and what do I get for my achievements?"

"Ignored?"

"Worse," Francis spat. "Jibes and insults. Inferior intellects spouting nonsense unworthy of my consideration."

I noticed he had worked himself into quite a state for someone who didn't care what his peers thought.

Rose coughed and interrupted his rant.

"The hellion?" she asked. "Can you determine the cause of death?"

"We're going to see him now," Francis answered, keeping his eyes glued to mine. "From my initial assessment, he didn't die from blunt force trauma."

Rose almost looked disappointed. "What do you mean?"

Francis broke his stare.

"According to my calculations and the notes provided by my people, the hellion was dead before he was introduced into *The Dirty Goblin*, specifically the ironwood bar in *The Dirty Goblin*."

This only confirmed what we had discovered earlier. Henry had been killed in the car. We just didn't know why.

"How much time?" I asked. "How much time before?"

"What do I look like? A mage? Best I can tell he's been dead for six to seven hours."

"That meant he was killed somewhere else and brought to the bar," I said, mostly to myself. "He didn't die in the car."

"Your powers of deduction are truly staggering," Francis said. "Amazing how you got to that conclusion by nearly repeating my exact words."

"What about the throw?" I asked, ignoring his jibe. "The hellion was thrown from the car, through a large plate glass window and into and over the ironwood bar."

Francis rubbed his chin in thought.

"Hellions are dense," he said, looking at Rose. "Some more than others. Judging from the impact, he was thrown at force. I'd be looking for a troll or something just as strong."

"I didn't notice another troll in the area, besides Percy," I said. "I know it wasn't Percy. He was behind the bar the whole time. Could they be using some kind of camouflage?"

"It's possible," Francis replied opening the door to one of the mortuary coolers. "Here we go. This is what's left of Henry the Hellion."

He pulled on the door and grabbed the movable tray. He took a second, scowled, and looked at the number of the cooler as if to confirm it was the correct number.

"What is it?"

I opened my coat so I could access my guns. My stomach did a little 'everything has just turned to shit' tango as I peeked in the cooler. A circle of runes covered the tray where the hellion should've been. I looked around for Henry but the cooler was empty.

Henry was gone.

"Where is he?" I asked, keeping my voice under control. "You sure this is the right cooler?"

Francis narrowed his eyes at me. "We do *not* misplace bodies in The Morgue."

"Are you saying Henry"—I pointed at the empty cooler—"went for a stroll? Maybe he felt it was too cramped in there and he wanted to stretch his legs?"

"Dragons are not known for their wit," Francis replied, "and now I know why."

"Where is he?" I countered, not sinking to playing his game. "How did he even get out?"

"I don't know, but he must still be in The Morgue," Francis said, reaching for a phone. "He needs to be contained. Take Fitz with you."

"Are you serious?" I laughed. "You want me to track down a semi-dead hellion in this frozen wasteland?"

"You're PPD, correct?" Francis asked, crossing his arms. "He means more to you than to me, right?"

"This is *your* morgue."

"Yes, and it's under *your* jurisdiction."

I turned to Rose who nodded slightly. "Technically The Morgue is Badlands PPD business," she agreed.

"Shit," I muttered under my breath and unholstered Butterfly.

The last thing I needed to be doing was demolishing parts of The Morgue.

"Fine," I said with a shrug. "Let's go find Henry."

CHAPTER 11

"*How* much of a killing machine is the average hellion?" I asked as we wandered down the corridors of The Morgue.

"Your first mistake," Rose answered, "is using the word average."

"Hellions are above average?"

She nodded. "Especially when compared to dragons. We are positively exceptional badasses."

"Aside from the badass ego you seem to possess," I said dryly, "what am I looking at?"

"Seriously?" she said. "You're sure you were raised in the Badlands?"

"I was," I said with a wave of my hand. "Just break it down for me."

We cleared a number of rooms, peeking into each in hopes of spotting our prey.

Based on the enormity of this place, I had the feeling it was going to take hours, if not days, to find him.

Obviously, I had no desire to wait that long, but maybe that was the norm for cops in the PPD.

Honestly, I had no idea.

I was green. A rookie. A noob.

Yet, here I was in charge of it all.

"We're faster, stronger, more ruthless, and, judging from my recent exposure to dragons," Rose explained, "several orders of magnitude smarter than the *average* dragon."

"Hilarious," I deadpanned. "Rose, what I'm asking is more along the lines of whether or not hellions possess a refractory death sleep?"

She stared at me for a second.

"That's actually a good question. To my knowledge, no. Once a hellion is dead, we stay dead."

I stopped at the intersection of the next corridor. I took a moment to assess the situation. Behind us, Fitz lumbered to a stop. I glanced over at him and shuddered reflexively. The combination of several races spliced together unnerved my senses in a visceral way.

"Did you see the runes?" I asked.

Rose nodded. "Were you able to decipher them?"

"Partially" —I stepped away from Fitz and lowered my voice—"it looked like a containment circle. At least from what I could tell. Do you think, Francis—"

"Don't know," Rose answered in the same tone, "but hellions don't just get up and start walking around after being launched head first into an ironwood bar. Something is off here and we need to figure out what, fast."

Another glance back at Fitz made me wonder exactly

how sentient he was. From what I could, tell he was non-verbal except for grunts and groans, but he seemed to understand the instructions Francis gave him.

Rose was right, though. We were racing against time.

House Mal would send another representative to The Morgue, one who wouldn't be as easily deterred as Sinclair.

She knew this world better than I did, though. "How soon before House Mal sends over a representative?"

"After your little run in with Sinclair, they won't send a representative," Rose answered, looking around the corner carefully before waving us forward.

"Really?"

She nodded. "They'll send a squad of security personnel posing as representatives to retrieve Henry's body. Probably send Sinclair again, the little shit."

"But we don't have Henry's body."

"Your powers of observation are off the charts," she shot back. "Of course, we don't have Henry. When they come to collect him—"

"We won't be able to produce the diplomat's body, which will give House Mal—"

"Cause to overreact."

"Which will be the catalyst for an 'incident', won't it?" I asked, seeing where the chain of events led.

Oh, what a web we weave.

It was obvious that this was a world I was not raised in. I mean, technically, I *was* raised in the Badlands...a portion of it, anyway. But that wasn't the same thing. *This* world was one of politics, organized crime, and likely worse.

It was all a game to them.

A serious game, certainly, but a game nonetheless.

"All this to stop the new chief of the PPD?" I asked in disbelief. "Isn't this taking the funeral party a little far?"

"Welcome to the Badlands," she chuckled. "Someone wants *you* out of the way in a permanent way, and they are going through some serious channels to do it." She was pointing at my chest. "Expected, and pretty damn normal considering they do this every time we get a new chief." Then she lowered her finger and shook her head. "Still, raising a hellion is *not* a basic spell. We are looking at serious necromancy here. That makes me think this isn't completely about the PPD."

What else would it be about?

It's not like I knew people here, aside from the valkyries, of course, and I doubted they'd put anything like this together.

Then again, maybe?

They *were* always testing me. From day one, in fact. I'll never forget my twentieth birthday party, which consisted of me undergoing emergency surgery six times due to their form of celebration. Some cultures spank, valkyries stab.

But, no, I was considered a member of their flock now. To hire out someone to kill me would not only go counter to that, it wouldn't be honorable.

"I haven't had time to make enemies," I reminded her. "This is my first day."

"You're a dragon," Rose answered quietly. "Kind of comes with the territory."

"Shit." She was right. It was easy to forget what you

really were when you had been raised by another culture. "Maybe I shouldn't have taken this job."

"Smartest thing you've said all day."

It wasn't like I'd had much of a choice, though.

My mother put me here. Well, my valkyrie mother. She said that there was a plan for me and that I needed to follow that plan.

Unfortunately, she never detailed quite what the plan was.

Somehow, though, I doubted it included me being on the other end of a hit.

"We're going to need a mage or undead tracker of some kind," I said, fighting to pull my confidence back up.

"Yeah, we're definitely going to need help." Rose looked back at Fitz. "And not the creature smorgasbord Francis sent with us. We're going to need the rest of the squad."

"Connectors?" I said, tapping the side of my head. "We can call them."

Rose shook her head. "The Morgue is shielded inside and out. Connectors are useless. We'll need to get outside to call them."

"Fine," I said. "We'll do that. Then we find Henry, get back to Francis and figure out who raised him. At the very least, Francis must know who has this ability."

"I can't let you do that, Chief," said a voice from behind us. "Your trip to The Morgue was meant to be one way."

I turned to face another hellion.

Where Sinclair was pomp and fluff, this one was hard edges and death. This guy was dressed simply in black leathers and held a large blade in one hand. His hair was cut short, giving him a boyish appearance until I looked into his eyes and saw the barely contained murderous intent.

This hellion was a lethal threat.

"Fuck me," Rose whispered. Then, she stood her ground. "What are you doing here, Croft?"

"I'm here representing the interests of House Mal," Croft replied. "They didn't appreciate your treatment of Emissary Sinclair."

"Bullshit," Rose shot back. "Who hired you?"

"Does it matter?"

"It will—when I'm done." Rose's voice cut through the frost like a blade. "I'll want to pay my respects to whoever thought I was such easy prey."

Croft smiled, and shook his head as he entered a fighting stance.

"You know that I can't tell you who hired me," he said. "but it won't matter in a few seconds anyway. You two, and the patchwork assistant need to end here"—he looked around The Morgue—"I'd say that's fitting."

"Well, then," I said, chambering a round in Butterfly, "come end us."

CHAPTER 12

*H*ellions move fast.

In half a second, Croft slid back down the corridor, putting enough distance between us that he was out of the range of my shotgun. Considering hellions are demons mixed with dragon blood, it didn't surprise me, but the move was hardly strategic.

"Your dragon thinks he's indestructible?" Croft asked, looking at Rose and pointing at me with his blade. "Maybe you want to educate him?"

I couldn't reach him with Butterfly from where I stood, but he couldn't reach me with his blade either. I took aim and was about to unleash the wrath of Butterfly anyway when Rose appeared in front of me, blocking my shot.

"What are you doing?" I asked.

She glared at me. "What are *you* doing?"

"Well, the plan was to pull the trigger and see if any of the projectiles struck the naughty hellion over there," I answered. "I *think* a few may, but it'd be a lot easier to test my theory if you moved."

She brought a hand down on Butterfly, forcing it to point down to the floor. "Do you realize what you're about to do?"

"Didn't I just cover that?"

"I'm talking about the deeper point of what you're doing," she grumbled.

"Oh, that. Uh…let's go with ridding the Badlands of one annoying hellion." I lifted the muzzle of Butterfly slowly as she resisted. "It may end up being two annoying hellions if you don't move, though."

She frowned at me.

"Doesn't it seem odd that he pulled a blade instead of a gun?" she asked. "You can't possibly be this suicidal…or stupid."

"Maybe I'm both?" I said. "One thing is for certain, it makes me question the whole 'hellions are smarter' thing though."

"We're in The Morgue, genius," she stated.

"Now who's being obvious?"

I tried to move her out of the way but she wouldn't budge. I was beginning to understand that hellions were stronger than they appeared.

"This place is filled with pentafluroethane," Rose pointed out.

"Well, why didn't you say so before?" I asked, acting as though I knew what she was talking about.

I didn't.

"You know what pentafluroethane is?" she asked, looking surprised.

"Honestly, it doesn't ring a bell. Should I be concerned?"

Her judging squint was probably enough of a response, but she continued on anyway. "It's used to keep all of the bodies in a frozen state. It's in the coolers and traces of it is in the air all around us. It's a refrigerant."

"Thank you for the lesson on how the coolers work," I said. "Now, if you could just let me in on how that affects my ability to shoot at Mr. Dicknose over there, I'll be happy to—"

"Pentafluroethane is a *flammable* refrigerant, you walnut."

"A *what?*" I asked, starting to make the connection. "Did you say flammable?"

"Oh your ears *do* work," she said. "For a moment, I thought they were just decoration."

"What the fu—?"

"We are standing in the largest bomb in the Badlands," she replied calmly. "You fire that shotgun and that'll be the last time you get to shoot your load."

"Phrasing," I muttered, taking in the scene.

Behind Rose and down the corridor, Croft waved his blade at me and gave me a one finger salute.

"Well, fuck me," I grumbled, holstering Butterfly. "What insane psychopath thought that was a good idea?"

She motioned behind us at Fitz.

"Same one who thought splicing a goblin, troll, and valkyrie into one body made sense," she said. "Francis made sure no one would fire a weapon in The Morgue without taking themselves out of the equation."

"And everyone else, apparently."

"Indeed."

"Your blade please," I said, holding out my hand as I glanced at her thigh sheaths.

She carried two long swords about the length of my forearm. There was one strapped to each leg.

"Excuse me?" she laughed, taking a step back. "These aren't just for decoration, dragon. They take years of practice to master, and I can assure you that Croft has mastered his."

"Give me your blade," I repeated, letting the anger seep into my voice. "I'll make sure to get it back to you...one way or another. You just pointed out that I can't use my guns, which means cutlery is the only option."

"Not really, there's always the option of being cut to shreds by a *trained* hellion," she said, glancing at Croft. "That'd be me, if you were wondering."

"I was."

"Croft is dangerous," she continued. "He's been trained by some of the best hellions in the Badlands."

I kept my hand out. "Nifty. Your blade please?"

"Honestly, I don't think your dragon training will help you here," she replied unsheathing her blade with a look of worry. "I know for a fact the lower temperature is probably affecting you by now." She began to turn. "Just let me deal with him."

"Who said I was trained by dragons?" I asked, reaffirming my desire to hold the blade. She placed it in my hand hilt first. I nodded. "Whatever happens, don't interfere."

"Interfere?" she scoffed. "This is going to be the fastest promotion in my career. Not that I want the job, but ten bucks is ten bucks." She shook her head at me. "Enjoy your funeral."

I focused and scaled my skin.

It took a little more energy than I was used to, which made me realize that Rose was right. The cold in The Morgue was a real factor.

But I had a hopeful ace up my sleeve. If Rose made the mistake of assuming dragons trained me, maybe Croft did too.

Dragons didn't teach me combat, valkyries did. They'd shown me the basics of how dragons fought, but only after years of tutelage in the valkyrie methods. Translation: fighting like a dragon was weird.

I hefted the blade in my hand as I looked at Croft. The weapon had perfect balance. I wouldn't expect less from Rose.

Hilda the Terror, the woman—and I use that term loosely—who trained and raised me, had me holding a blade the day I'd met her. It became an extension of my person. I just hadn't expected to need one at my new job. They seemed to be an antiquated means of taking down bad people. Guns were more efficient.

Lesson learned.

Scales covered every inch of my skin, but I didn't dare unleash more of my dragon form in a flammable environment. As far as I knew, I didn't possess ice powers, even though I knew ice dragons existed.

Valkyries were masters of close quarter bladed combat, and that meant *I* was a master of it as well.

Croft may have been taught by the best hellions, but the fiercest valkyrie in the Badlands taught me.

Having a blade in my hand was comfortable.

It felt like home.

Hilda's words came back to me:

Bladed combat is intimate, personal. Step in close, thrust first and fast. Use your wits, strength, guile, and remember your training. Don't think...act.

A grin formed on my lips, telling me that I was facing a dead hellion.

He just didn't know it yet.

CHAPTER 13

I stood still and focused my breathing as Croft
walked down the corridor toward me.

Rose cursed.

I glanced back and saw two more hellions had
appeared.

She unsheathed her other blade.

"You good?" I asked, focusing on Croft, who smiled as
he closed the distance.

"I'm not just good," Rose muttered. "I'm the best and
right now I'm pissed."

"Try to keep one of them alive," I said. "We need to
find out who sent them."

"This is the work of House Mal," Rose replied.
"Specifically that little sniveling worm, Sinclair. I can't kill
him, but I can make him hurt. And he *will* hurt once I'm
done here."

Something about the way Croft was moving gave me
pause.

I knew he was underestimating me, but I was starting

to get the feeling that I may have been doing the same to him.

"Any tips on fighting a hellion?" I said, shifting into a defensive fighting stance. "You know, like stab him in a specific spot so he'll die immediately?"

"Tips," she said with a short laugh. "Sure, just one. When you fight a hellion you have to be more."

"Be more? Really?" I sniffed at that. "That's really helpful in a vague obscure Zen way. Should I wonder how wet is a drop of water?"

"Only if you're an idiot," she shot back "Be more ferocious, more ruthless, and more lethal than he is and you *may* have a chance at surviving more than ten seconds."

"Is that all?" I asked. "When you put it that way—"

"Quit yapping and do as I say," she said, walking away, blade in hand, as she faced the other hellions. "If you don't, I'll make sure you get the appropriate PPD burial ceremony a chief deserves."

"I'm not dead yet," I said, and tapped into more of my dragon power.

Croft leapt into the air and stepped off one wall of the corridor, leading with a downward thrust.

His attack forced me back as I parried.

Okay, this guy was even quicker than I'd thought. He'd damn near taken off one of my fingers.

"What kind of dragon are you?" he sneered and dodged to the side as I lunged forward. He cackled as he moved out of range. "Pathetic. Do you even know how to wield a blade?"

"Come on and find out, asshole."

His smile dissolved.

With a burst of speed, he slashed on a diagonal, pushing me to the side as I avoided his blade. I ducked under a horizontal swipe, landing me right in the path of a front kick that launched me down the corridor.

I landed with a groan.

The kick was more of a shock than actual damage, but I had to be careful. He was faster than any enemy I had faced in the past. Even though I sparred with my valkyrie teachers with live blades, I never got the impression they were trying to actively kill me. Cut me, yes, but not kill me.

Croft wasn't just trying to cut me, he *was* trying to kill me.

I felt for the ring around my finger. It was the only jewelry I wore and it allowed me the ability to tap into a heaping dose of dragon power without going full dragon.

I couldn't use it yet, though, I had to wait until he thought I was vulnerable.

Croft slid forward again, leading with his blade.

I barely stepped back in time. My scales deflected the point of his attack off my abdomen as he rotated around me and executed a crushing knife-hand strike at my neck.

I brought my arm up in time to parry the strike and felt every bone in my body vibrate from the blow. He slashed low at my leg and I rolled back avoiding the attack, holding my blade in front of my body as I crouched.

"You've never fought a hellion," Croft said as we circled each other. "You're outclassed and outmatched. If you surrender now, I promise you a quick death."

"That's a real generous offer, but I'm going to have to pass." But he was right. If I kept playing against him in my current state, I'd be toast within a minute. I expanded my senses and placed a finger on my ring. It was dangerous, but so was fighting Croft. "But if *you'd* like to surrender, I promise to prosecute to the full extent of the law and extend you fair treatment."

"You fool," Croft shot back with a laugh. "There's only one law in the Badlands: kill or be killed."

He crouched down and leapt forward.

I pressed my ring and ducked.

The energy contained deep within my body, channeled by my tattoo and pressing of the ring, unleashed a very specific component of my dragon form.

My wings.

I caught Croft mid-air and slammed him into the side of the corridor, face-first.

He stumbled off the wall, shaken.

My wings were nearly indestructible extensions of my body. They gave me speed and agility that made Croft look like a slug.

I skip-stepped forward and buried my blade in his chest. His eyes opened in shock as he realized what had just happened. My wings retracted and disappeared as I reined in some of the power.

"What happened to fair treatment?" Croft gurgled as he slid down the wall behind him. "I thought you were sworn to uphold the law."

"I am," I replied at his sunken form, "but in your case I've decided to enforce the law of the Badlands."

He looked down at his wound, his breathing ragged.

"You're going to fit right in with the Badlands," he said with a short laugh and then started coughing up blood. After a few seconds the coughing stopped. "I can honestly say you surprised me."

"It's clear you've never faced a dragon."

"You didn't..." He choked and sputtered for a moment. "You didn't fight like a dragon."

"Because I wasn't raised by dragons," I whispered as I leaned in, giving him a wink. "I was raised by valkyries."

I removed the blade from his chest and glanced over at Rose and Fitz. They had already dispatched the hellions they faced.

Rose approached with a look of admiration on her face.

Fitz was missing an arm, an ear, and one eye. He didn't seem all that bothered by it.

"Who?" Rose asked Croft as she crouched in front of him. "Who in House Mal?"

Croft laughed and sputtered blood. "Fuck you, Rose."

She held out her hand without looking at me. I placed the blade hilt first in it.

"Last time, Croft. Who hired you?"

He spat in her direction. "Fu—"

Croft never finished his sentence. His head sailed down the corridor as Rose slashed and sheathed her blade in one smooth motion.

"Is he going to stay dead?" I asked, remembering that we were looking for another hellion that was supposed to be dead. "I don't feel like facing him again."

"How did you do that with the wings?" she asked,

ignoring my question. "I've never seen a dragon form wings in human form."

For a split second, I considered not telling her, but if she was to be my second-in-command, I needed to establish trust. I held up my hand and showed her the ring. It was a series of valkyrie chainmail links connected to form a ring. They had imbued it with latent power giving me the ability to channel my dragon energy through it.

"*Whoosh,*" I said. "This ring lets me control my wings without going full dragon."

"And you named this ring, Whoosh?"

"Great name, right?" I said. "You know, because the sound my wings make when they appear...whoosh."

"You mean it's not the sound a coherent thought makes when it escapes that thing you call a brain?"

I gave her a hurt look. "You don't like it?"

She gave me a withering glare.

"Let's go find Henry," she said as she walked down the corridor away from what used to be Croft.

CHAPTER 14

*W*e ran down the corridors. Well, Rose and I ran, Fitz did a quick shuffle. He was surprisingly fast for someone who was falling apart.

"Keep it together, Fitz," Rose yelled out behind us, "and stay close. Chief, can you sense Henry?"

"I'm a valkyrie-raised dragon not a bloodhound," I said as we stopped at another intersection. "Besides he's dead—"

"Undead," Rose interjected. "Henry is undead and we better find him fast."

"What's the rush?" I asked. "It's not like he's going to escape The Morgue."

"Do you really think House Mal would send only Croft and two more hellions?" Rose asked looking behind us. "He was the warning shot. It's only a matter of time before they start using the big guns."

"Big guns?"

"Every House has a guard," Rose said, heading down

the corridor to our right. "Weren't you taught this growing up? Anyway the House guard—"

"Is that like a gatekeeper?"

"Not really," she answered as we slowed our pace. "The guard is an elite squad of fighters who protect the House in case of attack or an attempted destruction by another House."

"Hellions try to destroy other Houses?"

"On very rare occasions," Rose said. "It requires approval by other Houses, is usually a collaborative effort, and requires the complete eradication of every member of the House being taken down."

"Can they do that?"

"As long as they eliminate every last member of the House within the allotted time, yes."

"And if they fail to do so?"

"Then the last remaining member of the targeted House can then lay claim to the attacking House, or Houses, as the case may be."

"Wow," I said, shaking my head as we turned a corner.

"It's efficient, ruthless, and brutal," Rose said with a smile, drawing one of her blades and handing it to me. "Only the strong and intelligent survive. A dragon wouldn't understand."

I took the blade and frowned at her. "Nice."

"Thanks."

"Do *you* sense him?" I asked.

She nodded. "And you should, too. You aren't a valkyrie, Chief. You're a dragon. Start using the senses you have." She looked down at the blade she handed me.

"And if we make it back to the PPD headquarters, get your own damn blade."

I wanted to reply with something snarky, but she was right.

If I didn't start tapping into my inner dragon, my tenure as chief of the Badlands PPD would be over before I was a week in.

My failure would only earn me Hilda's wrath, assuming I lived long enough.

The last thing I needed was to face my adoptive mother's caress of mercy, which consisted of a gauntleted backhand slap across the floor. These gems usually occurred the instant I made a mistake with any technique.

I called it the caress of mercy because, before training me, she used to fix mistakes with the point of her blade.

Most valkyries never made it through basic training without repeated infirmary visits.

Again, I bring to note my birthday party as a case in point of how valkyries handled celebrations. Imagine what training was like.

We turned another corner and came face to face with the recently deceased Henry.

CHAPTER 15

*H*enry was having an especially bad day. I'm sure that the last thing he imagined when he started this day was that he'd be killed, propelled through a plate glass window and into an ironwood bar. To top that off, someone or something had brought him back from recently deceased.

"Hey, Henry," I said, slowly approaching the swaying figure at the other end of the corridor.

The cold was seeping into my bones and making me sluggish. I would've given anything for a warm fire right about now. As long as it didn't include exploding myself into small dragon bits.

Henry was blue.

Not sad, but the actual color.

Then again, I imagine he was probably sad, too.

He swayed back and forth and kept a lazy gaze on us as we shifted into position around him.

He raised one arm and pointed down the corridor at us.

"You need to die," he rasped. "I can't let you live."

"I think he's talking to you," Rose said under her breath, unsheathing her other blade.

"He could just as easily mean you," I hissed back. "You don't exactly have a fan club."

Rose pointed an index finger at me.

"Chief."

Then she pointed the same finger to her chest.

"Not chief."

She lowered her hand.

"Pretty sure he means you."

Okay, so she had me there.

"Can you tell us who killed you, Henry?" I asked as he shambled in our direction. "Do you remember?"

At the very least, I was hoping to get some information about who would want to start civil war in the Badlands. It's possible there was enough of Henry in this corpse that he could tell us something useful.

"Killed me?" Henry slurred. "Who said I...I was dead?"

"Oh, Henry," Rose said. "I have some real bad news for you."

"Wait," I said, holding out a hand. "He doesn't think he's dead. Maybe he can tell us who's behind this."

Rose rolled her eyes and shrugged, motioning toward the undead hellion as she took a step back.

"Henry," I said, waving a hand and getting his somewhat divided attention. "Can you remember today? Do you recall what happened?"

A look of confusion flitted across Henry's face.

"I started my morning," Henry began, looking up as if remembering. "I left my home..."

He placed a hand on the wall, doubling over as he grimaced, gripping his chest with his other hand. This surprised me. I didn't know the undead could feel pain. Rose grabbed my arm in a vise-like grip and yanked me back.

"Run!" she hissed in my face, grabbing Fitz and shoving him at Henry. "Run, now!"

"Help...help me," Henry reached out, snagging Fitz's only available arm. "The pain. It's too much."

I stood there transfixed looking past Fitz at the pleading Henry.

"Since when do the undead feel..." I started as Rose grabbed me again and pulled me away from Henry and Fitz.

"We need to move—now," she rasped and I heard the undercurrent of fear. "He's carrying a blood bomb."

The terror in her voice kickstarted my brain, which sent an urgent memo to my feet about picking up the pace and getting my ass away from an undead hellion carrying whatever a blood bomb was.

I started running fast when I felt the decompression in The Morgue, followed by a low *thwump* behind me. I turned to look back and saw that Fitz had come apart at the seams—literally. Whatever was left of him was all over the corridor.

Henry lay on the floor, finally dead.

Blood was everywhere and it was coalescing.

"What the hell is that?" I asked.

"Close," Rose said, next to me.

"What?" I said, thinking her response made zero sense.

"Blood bomb means blood imps," she replied, studying

the area like an animal who was on the menu. "They're not from hell, precisely, but they damn sure could be."

"Oh, right," I said, blinking. "What are blood imps again?"

"Hungry creatures who attack any living thing in proximity." She spun and stared at me with crazed eyes. "They'll eat your face if you stand still. Now move!"

CHAPTER 16

"Unleashing a bomb full of blood imps that will attack any living thing inside of a morgue isn't a coincidence," I said as we raced back to Francis. "This was a coordinated attack."

"Figure that out all on your own now, did you?" Rose shot back as she picked up the pace and pointed ahead. "Down that corridor."

I glanced quickly behind us and noticed the small pinpricks of light in the frost of The Morgue. The amount of lights was disconcerting, especially when I realized they were moving and closing on our position.

"These blood imps," I said, catching up to Rose as she ran, "do they have glowing eyes?"

"Glowing eyes, about six inches tall, and a mouth full of razor sharp teeth," she answered, taking the next left. "Do not let them get close to you, unless you want to be lunch."

"So land piranhas?"

"With glowing eyes, yes."

"Best way to get rid of them?" I asked as she headed down another corridor.

"I'm doing it," she answered as she kept her legs churning.

That made me assume that running away as fast as possible was the best defense against blood imps. Kind of made me feel sorry for anyone who got in their way. Then again, it *did* seem they were only interested in us.

"Do you even know where we're going?" I asked, though my breath was becoming somewhat labored at this point.

I only asked because she had led us into a dead end. We stood in a slightly narrow corridor. I noticed a large groove in the floor at the intersection as we entered the space.

"Of course I know where we're going," she said, as the sound of growling grew closer. Rose licked her lips and pointed at my shoulder. "Those wings of yours, how strong are they?"

"I don't know what you mean." The look on her face gave me the feeling I *did* know what she meant. "Are you asking if I can lift—"

"How fireproof?" she interrupted, with a quick glance at the ceiling. "Fully or just flame resistant?"

"I'm a dragon," I answered, but even I wasn't positive. "I would imagine pretty resistant?"

She walked to the center of the floor and stood directly under a large vent in the ceiling.

"You wanted to know how to get rid of blood imps?" she said, looking up at the vent grill directly above us.

The sound had switched from a low growling to a

high-pitched grinding. It reminded me of the sound two sharp pieces of metal made when hitting each other.

It made me wince.

"What is that?" I groaned, covering my ears. "Does Francis have machinery down here or something?"

"No. That's the sound of teeth."

"Teeth?" I dropped my hands. "What do you mean teeth?"

"Blood imps," she said, without taking her eyes off the ceiling while moving another step to the right. "Told you, hungry creatures that attack any living thing in proximity and will eat your face if you stand still."

"So they're *not* just here for us?"

"We're the only living things within proximity, Chief. Was I not clear about that?"

I nodded. "What's not clear is how to erase them," I answered. "I think that would be valuable information to have right now."

She didn't look all that interested in dropping into a dissertation regarding blood imps at the moment.

"Just the quick version, if you please."

"Whoever unleashed the blood bomb on us, timed it so it would go off in Henry while we were in The Morgue." Rose answered, drawing one of her guns. "A funeral party I can understand, but like you said before, this was a little too coordinated for that. Add the containment rune and we're dealing with an entirely different element."

At least we were on the same page as far as that went. So far I'd felt as though I wasn't getting up to speed on anything.

The problem I had at the moment was the fact that

Rose, the very person who yelled at me about even thinking about using my sawed-offs in The Morgue, was holding a very ominous weapon of her own.

"What are you doing?" I said, looking at the handcannon she held. "You told me this place was a bomb waiting to go off."

"It is," she said with a smile that immediately let me know she was up to something unpleasant. My valkyrie trainers used to give me the same smile right before inflicting several painful wounds. "Can you take one step over please? Thank you."

"What about the pentafloro—refrigerant? The *flammable* refrigerant?"

"We're going to do the one thing they won't expect," Rose answered, still wearing the smile of impending doom.

I was beginning to realize that not all hellions were crazy—just my second-in-command.

"You never told me how to deal with blood imps," I said, seeing the flickering lights of their eyes in the distance. "*Now* would be a good time."

She stepped close and moved me over slightly to one side while looking up. I followed her gaze and saw the vent grill above us.

"How often can you form your wings?"

"There's no limit as long as I have access to my dragon energy. Why?"

"Good," she said with a nod. "When I tell you, form your wings and wrap them around us."

"Listen, Rose," I said, putting my hands up as she wrapped an arm around my waist. "I know that in times of stress and near death, feelings can be formed between two people—"

She brought the muzzle of the gun under my chin. "If you finish that sentence, I'll feed what's left of you to the imps."

I shut up.

For a second anyway.

"I was just," I continued reflexively, "you know I don't want to get things confused between the two of us. We have to work as professionals here."

"When I tell you," she growled in response, "activate your wings and wrap them around us, clear?"

"Clear," I said with a nod.

I spotted the imps getting closer. Their flashing eyes bounced in the frost of The Morgue as they jumped and surged down the corridors at us.

She waited until all of them had entered the corridor.

When the last one had stepped past the groove in the floor, she raised an arm, looked at me, and fired at the grill opening.

It imploded.

She then turned and fired the next round into the blood imps.

"Now!" she yelled, tightening her grip around my waist.

I was momentarily deaf from the discharge, but I got the signal.

I pressed Whoosh and felt the energy surge from the ring into the tattoo and throughout my body. My scales appeared an instant later as the mass of blood imps surged toward the end of the corridor.

My wings flared around our bodies as I felt Rose tense in my arms.

A plume of flame formed in the center of the blood imps and spread.

Behind the imps, a large steel door slammed down sealing us in the corridor. In a few seconds, we were going to be barbecued.

"What the—"

"Keep them around us," Rose yelled. "I don't feel like getting scorched in here."

Above us, the vent kicked on and I felt air being sucked out of the space. Rose crouched slightly keeping her grip around my waist and pushed up off the floor.

CHAPTER 17

*W*e landed in the ventilation shaft as a fireball chased us up.

The warmth of the flames caressed my wings as we bounced off the top of the shaft and landed unceremoniously in the vent itself. I raised my wings as a barrier against the second wall of flame that filled the ventilation system as the fire was siphoned out of the space we'd stood in seconds earlier.

"Fire," Rose said, sitting up, dusting herself off, and catching her breath. "*That* is the best way to deal with blood imps. Seems like your wings are flame resistant. We should see if that holds true for the rest of you." She studied me for a moment. "Seriously, I think we should test what kind of impact your scales can take. Are they flame resistant too?"

I held up a hand and leaned against the cramped shaft wall. The cool metal of the vent shaft felt good against my cheek.

"Let's hold off on 'scorch the dragon' tests, thank you."

My wings had retracted moments after the second wall of flame dissipated, but it would take a minute or two for me to recover. Still, I was glad they had protected us from the inferno that had raged around us before. I had no desire to learn empathy for a marshmallow at a campfire.

Rose shrugged. "We can do it later. It's good info to have in any case." Rose pursed her lips. "I'm sure Nimble would be interested in the test results."

"Yeah," I said with a heavy dose of sarcasm, "I'm sure he would. Maybe we can just ask him *what* he added to my tattoos? It could be he already knows the extent of the adaptations, right?"

"That's actually not a bad idea," she said after a few seconds as she rubbed her chin. "Or, we could just blast you with explosives until they hurt?"

"I'll go with the non-explosive option, thanks."

She held up a hand. "Just trying to help. Nothing like immediate feedback in my opinion."

Her 'immediate feedback' plan sounded like she was just interested in trying to blow me to pieces.

I peeked down the opening to the floor below. Nothing but ash remained of the blood imps. The stench of burnt flesh wafted up into the vent and made me cough.

"You'll get used to it," Rose said, her voice grim. "Plenty of things burn in the Badlands. After a while, the smell of burnt flesh won't bother you much."

"Don't know what's worse," I said, staring at her. "That burning flesh is common in the Badlands or that you're used to it."

She shrugged.

"Badlands PPD: We protect, we serve, and we deter."

"Protect and serve I understand. Deter? That involve pre-emptive policing?"

"We have a 'shoot them before they shoot you' type of policy," Rose said. "I don't enjoy being target practice."

"You literally just suggested that *I* be used for target practice!"

"Yes," she replied slowly. "Keyword is 'you,' Chief, not me."

"I'll keep that in mind," I said with a dark look.

Okay, so that meant that nobody was really on my side in the PPD. Or, if Rose *was* on my side, she had an interesting way of showing it.

Yes, she'd taught me how to avoid being chewed to death by the blood imps, but that was likely just because *I* was her only hope at surviving their mass of teeth, too. If she could have found a quick exit, I'd probably be a meal sitting in a bunch of tiny stomachs right now.

Whatever.

I had to keep my focus.

Getting any more irritated than I already was wouldn't help me in the least.

"This isn't just a funeral party, is it?" I asked her.

She shook her head.

"The goblin greet made sense. Every chief gets some variation of that." She was glancing around again. "The hellion resurrection was some next level hate, though. The fact that House Mal sent Croft to dust me along with you is insulting." She stopped scanning and gave me a look. "No offense."

"None taken," I grunted. "I think."

"They've acted against officers of the PPD," she said her voice dark. "We can't let that go unanswered or every piece of scum in the Badlands will think they can just attack us without consequence."

"Assuming they're not just targeting the chief, right?"

"I thought that was a given."

Yay.

"Anyway," I continued, "when you say we can't let that go unanswered, you mean we need to apprehend, arrest, and prosecute, right?"

"Or, we can unleash retribution and spread their lifeless corpses up and down the Strip as a sign to anyone else who would dare attack an officer of the PPD."

"Wait," I laughed. "You want to wage a war on every criminal in the Badlands?"

"Unrelenting and unmerciful violence is the only language they understand," she stated, her voice laced with lethal intent. "The sooner you wrap your head around that, Chief, the more likely you'll survive the week."

Regardless of her personal stance on the issue, there was the case of simple logistics.

"Badlands PPD doesn't have enough personnel for all-out war," I answered, after taking a long breath. "How about arresting those responsible for Henry's death?"

"We can start there," she agreed, staring at me. "After we find them—then we go to war."

"Or," I said, grabbing her arm, "just an idea, here, what say we uphold the law and make the Badlands a safer place for everyone?"

She smiled as the ventilation system shut down and then reversed the flow. I heard the steel blast door beneath us slide out of the opening.

"*That* is a wonderful dream," she replied, plucking my hand away. "For now, though, what say we go have some words with Francis?"

Rose grabbed the edge of the opening and flipped forward and out, landing cat-like on the floor below.

"Good idea," I said, admiring the landing.

While I harbored serious reservations about Rose, she *had* managed to lift both of us up out of a wall of flame, and into an opening barely large enough for us to fit. Her skills were impressive, and she was definitely an asset that I needed to rely on.

But I was still the chief. That meant I needed to establish the chain of command as soon as possible, and my being new to this couldn't stand in the way of it.

I was still chief.

Damn it.

I leaned out and jumped down.

Now, I'd like to think I landed just as gracefully when I jumped out of the ventilation system. The reality was closer to landing and almost losing my balance as I bounced off the wall on my right.

"You okay?" Rose asked, looking me over. "That was about as agile as a brick."

"No one said being a PPD chief required acrobatics," I grumbled. "I thought this was going to be mostly a desk job."

"Desk job?" she scoffed as she headed down the

corridor. "The only time a Badlands PPD chief is behind a desk is if he or she is using the desk to stop bullets."

I cracked my back.

"I'm starting to get that."

"Good, the sooner you do, the longer you'll stay alive."

Rose was really starting to confuse me. Did she want me dead or alive?

"I thought you wanted a promotion?"

"No amount of money is worth the bullseye you have on your back," she said with a shake of her head. "Besides, this way I can do what needs to be done and you can take the blame..." She coughed and looked up at me. "Erm, I mean the responsibility."

"Just keep walking," I muttered.

We arrived at the main platform and climbed the stairs.

Francis stood on the platform and motioned for us to follow him. We walked to the other end and descended a long flight of wide steps before entering what I assumed to be his office.

He shut the door behind us and flicked a switch.

I immediately felt a buzzing sensation all over my skin.

"What the hell, Francis?" Rose burst out, slamming a fist on a nearby table.

"Literal or figurative?" Francis replied calmly. "Where is Fitz?"

"We nearly got *literally* chewed up by blood imps!"

"Blood imps?" Francis asked, pensively. "I don't recall storing blood imps in any of the coolers." He tapped on his keyboard and studied the screen for a moment. "Nope.

I wonder how they got inside The Morgue?" He glanced over at us with a hopeful look. "Did you save any? I'd love to examine one."

Rose glared at him.

"No, we did *not* save any," Rose stated. "Henry was carrying a blood bomb."

Yeah, he was, wasn't he? But how? Where would he have gotten it? He certainly didn't have it when he flew through the window of *The Dirty Goblin*.

"Guys," I said, "I doubt he was carrying the bomb while he was a missile at the Goblin."

Rose turned to Francis. "Someone working for you is dirty."

"Dear Rose, they're all dirty," Francis said with a smile. "You, of all people know that the Badlands isn't full of upstanding citizens, just varying degrees of dirt."

"Shit, he's right," Rose said. "Anyone could have placed the bomb."

"Good help is hard to find...which is why I make it," Francis answered. "Now, again, where is Fitzroy?"

"He was too close to Henry during the explosion," I said. "Fitz came undone...I mean he fell to pieces..." I paused and took a breath. "What I'm trying to say is that he's all over the corridor where Henry exploded."

"Understood," Francis said, holding up a finger and pressing a button near his desk. A few seconds later there was a knock on the door. Francis pressed another button and buzzed the armed guard into the office.

"Yes, Mr. Stein?"

"It seems Fitz has encountered a mishap," Francis said.

"Can you collect and bring him back, in addition to the hellion who went missing earlier today?"

"Will do, Mr. Stein," the guard said as he left the office.

"This wasn't a funeral party," Rose said once the door was closed. It was nice being right now and then. "Anyone could have placed the bomb, true. The circle took special knowledge, though." She was staring at Francis. "Who do you know who could cast a delayed resurrection from a circle?"

Francis sat behind his desk and steepled his fingers.

"I don't appreciate having The Morgue involved in politics," he said. "This is why I go to great lengths to limit violence within its walls."

"Tell that to House Mal and Croft," I grunted.

"Croft, the hellion assassin, is here?" Francis asked. "What is he doing here? Not that I'm not grateful for the steady business, but why would he be here?"

"He isn't any more," Rose answered. "At least not in one piece."

Couldn't argue with that. "Croft was sent here with two other hellions to finish us off."

Francis nodded slowly, a sinister grin forming on his face.

"It would seem you have made powerful enemies, Chief Phoenix," he said. "Sinclair and House Mal are not without their resources."

"Bullshit, Francis, and you know it," Rose said, leaning over the desk. For a second I thought she was going to crush the guy, but he seemed immune to Rose's power of intimidation. My respect for him went up a few notches.

"You know Croft wouldn't do a job for House Mal, no matter how much they paid him."

"But Croft said he was working with Mal, didn't he?" I asked, replaying the scene from earlier.

"He was lying," she replied, keeping her eyes on Francis.

"How do you know that he was—"

She shot me a look that said, 'Really?'

I gave her one back that said, 'Sorry.'

With a sigh, Rose refocused on Francis. "What mage cast the spell, Francis?"

"I would rather not get—" Francis started.

Rose moved faster than I could track, which is fast, considering my dragon senses can pretty much track anything.

She unsheathed one of her thigh blades, flipped it, and buried it several inches into Francis' desk, right in-between his arms.

"Are you about to tell me you would rather not get involved?" Rose asked, sweetly. "After I was frozen in your damn icebox, nearly killed by a hellion hit squad, and almost made into dinner for a bunch of hungry little fucking imps?" She leaned further in. "Is that *seriously* what you're about to tell me?"

She didn't raise her voice or change her inflection much, but the menace that came across dropped the temperature of the room by several degrees.

Francis' earlier demeanor of cool aloofness was starting to show some cracks. His face appeared paler than usual and a twitch developed under his right eye, but he stayed behind his desk looking as calmly as he could at Rose.

He was either very brave or very stupid.

"I'm going to tell you that while I'd rather not get myself or The Morgue involved, it would seem I *have* been involved against my will," Francis replied quietly. "This breach of protocol can erode the trust placed in The Morgue, and thus, I will and must take action."

What a swell guy.

"He's not related to Graffon, is he?" I said under my breath. Then, I asked directly, "Do you know who cast the circle?"

"The circle was a residual construct, meaning it entered The Morgue with Henry," Francis replied, removing Rose's blade and handing it back to her. "That means it was a mage. The window of opportunity was small and would have required fast casting."

"That actually makes sense," Rose said, her edge still fully present. "Whoever did this had to do it on the way here."

"Precisely," Francis agreed, and though it looked as if it took some effort, he added, "I examined the circle residue after we discovered it and found it to be from Mage Lowell."

CHAPTER 18

"*L*owell?" Rose asked. "Are you sure?"

"Within a one percent margin of error, yes" Francis replied with a nod as the armed guard buzzed the door again and wheelbarrowed the remains of Fitz into the office.

"This is all of him, Mr. Stein," the guard said, placing the wheelbarrow near one of the examination tables. "The hellion was sent to processing."

"Thank you. Are you certain you found every last bit?"

"Absolutely, he's all there," the guard answered. "Will you need anything else?"

"No, thank you," Francis answered with a wave of his hand as he focused on Fitz. "Oh, wait, there appears to be another group of hellions—" Francis glanced at Rose who held up three fingers "—three of them to be precise, in the corridor near Henry's final demise. Could you collect the bodies and send them to processing as well?"

"Sure thing, Mr. Stein. Anything else?"

"That's all for now, thank you."

The guard left the office silently.

"Who is Mage Lowell?" I asked, not liking Rose's expression.

"He works for Leon, and more specifically The Company," Rose answered. "He's sort of a magical cleaner. He's good, too."

"One of the best," agreed Francis.

Rose's shoulders dropped. "Shit."

"But we can trace him now, right?" I asked. "Francis was able to trace the runes back to him, yes?"

Rose shook her head and looked at Francis. "Tell him."

"Tell me what?" I asked, confused. "Francis just said he knows that Mage Lowell did it."

"I think it's best if I show him," Francis replied. "Follow me."

We walked back to the cooler that held Henry's body. In front of it stood two armed guards. They stepped to the side with a nod when Francis approached.

The area smelled like the corridor with the charred imps.

The exterior of the cooler was a blackened mess. The metal door was twisted, distorted, and hung from one hinge. Inside it was worse. The interior had been slagged. The metal tray that once held Henry's body was a mass of metal sitting inside a melted compartment.

"How did he manage to do this?" I asked, looking in wonder. "And how did this not blow up the entire morgue?"

"Both good questions," Francis replied with an impressed look. "Mage Lowell is adept at internal combustion. This example is similar to the blood bomb placed inside Henry, but without the imps."

That's when it hit me. "The circle?"

"Exactly," Francis said with a nod. "Wherever he places one of his containment circles, the surface temperature increases until—" he pointed at the cooler "—this is the result. With Henry, he added a delay component that would trigger the blood imps. It's quite elegant in its deviousness."

"So glad you're a fan," muttered Rose. "We can't prove Lowell did this, though. There's no evidence."

"This Mage Lowell guy can create circles that bring people back from the dead, yeah?" I asked, still trying to process the events of the last hour. "That would mean he's some kind of dark mage?"

"In the Badlands, you'll find that most of the mages dabble in darkness," Francis answered. "It's what makes the Badlands...the Badlands."

"Where is he now?" I asked, suddenly angry that this Company thought it could flagrantly break the law without consequences. "Is there a Company headquarters?"

Francis and Rose glanced at each other.

"You plan on bringing The Company to justice?" Francis asked raising an eyebrow. "Who do you plan on arresting?"

"Everyone, if I need to," I answered, still in a barely contained rage. "They can't get away with this."

"Get away with what?" Francis asked and looked at Rose again. "If you want him to last more than a week, you'd better educate him; If not, I'll prepare a cooler for his early retirement." He then giggled and pointed across the room to a cooler that read Chief Phoenix. "I'm kidding, I already have one ready."

I frowned at him.

Curbing his laughter, he pointed at the cooler that had previously housed Henry. "Once you're done collecting whatever evidence is left, let the guards know so I can repurpose the cooler."

"I'll take care of it," Rose said, grabbing me by the arm. "Have a good one, Francis. Thanks."

Francis waved a hand as he walked away lost in thought.

"He's just going to let this go?" I asked. "They almost blew up The Morgue."

"Technically, that was us."

"Shit, you're right. Well, what about the blood bomb and the melted compartment?"

Rose glanced at the guards near the door. "Let's get outside, get some fresh air, and finish this conversation there, okay?"

We stepped past The Morgue goons, and headed outside to the Hurricane.

The guards we walked by nodded to Rose, but held their rifles in the low, ready position.

They seemed on edge.

I guess guarding a building of potential undead would do that to anyone.

"We didn't even collect evidence," I said once we were inside the car. "At least we should have gathered the ash of the imps or something."

Rose ignored me and looked at the guards. "They seem twitchy to you?"

"If by twitchy you mean ready to unload a magazine into us—then yes, they seem twitchy."

"We aren't going to get close to Lowell without a reasonable deterrent," Rose said, starting the car.

The initial roar of the engine deafened me for a second.

Dragon senses.

I needed to be aware of my surroundings and adapt accordingly.

"Deterrent?" I asked as she sped away from The Morgue and my hearing returned. "What kind of deterrent is going to get us close to Lowell?"

"The kind that convinces The Company that it's more trouble to protect that piece of shit Mage than to turn him over to us," Rose replied with what I realized was her smile of impending destruction.

"Where are we going to get this deterrent?" I asked, nearly going scaled as she swerved in between two trucks.

"We need to see Wind, right after we swing by HQ."

CHAPTER 19

*T*he Badlands PPD was located at the edge of the city.

Rose's driving, and I use that term loosely to describe her minimal control of a high-powered vehicle down the streets of the Badlands, was interesting. Despite the white-knuckle, nausea inducing, stomach turning maneuvers she executed, I had to admit, getting us to the Badlands PPD HQ in one piece was an automotive feat of epic proportions. So, Rose was a badass when it came to driving, too.

I'd never admit it out loud, but it was true.

In general, she was just an all out threat...hopefully in a good way when all was said and done.

The Badlands PPD's one, and *only*, precinct was located in a large fortress-like building situated at the edge of town. The building itself sat on a small hill surrounded by hi-tech security measures. Access to the PPD was through a series of manned gates where we were required to present identification at each checkpoint.

It was my first time there. I'd been inside virtually a couple of times, but this was my maiden voyage into the building physically.

"Did they put the PPD out here for heightened security?" I asked after the third checkpoint. "I mean it makes sense, but why so many checkpoints?"

Rose retrieved her badge from the most recent guard.

"The Badlands PPD is placed out here for one reason and one reason only."

We drove past the guards and parked in the designated PPD parking area. I looked over to the side and saw another Hurricane parked under the sign that read 'PPD Chief.'

"To keep it away from the population?" I ventured.

"In the case of an all-out assault on the Badlands PPD, damage to the main Strip and city could be contained," Rose answered. "I've even heard a rumor that the entire place is rigged to blow as a contingency plan."

"What would require that kind of contingency?"

"Remind me to take you on a tour of Hell one day."

"Chief Phoenix and Lieutenant Rose," Nimble's voice came through my communicator, startling me, *"please visit the tech station. I'd like to discuss your recent activities if you don't mind."*

"What does he mean 'recent activities'?" I asked, taking in the activity of the precinct.

My prior visit was a whirlwind of procedure and paperwork, and it was all seen through the opposite side of a camera.

This time I was able to appreciate the level of excitement while being caught up in it directly.

"Don't stress it," Rose said with a wave of her hand. "Nimble always gets his panties tied up in knots. Probably wants to address your whizz."

"My whizz?"

"Yes, you know, the smush. That thing you do when you pull on yourself—the jizz."

"I'm not following," I said, cringing in disgust, "and I don't know if I want to at this point."

"That thing you do when your wings pop out? You know now that we're here, we should really test how combat ready those things are. Nimble said he has some spare rocket launchers no one is using. We could go down to the range—"

"My Whoosh?" I said, eager to change the conversation from being a rocket target. "The ring I'm wearing is called the Whoosh."

"That's what I said," Rose answered, taking the stairs down and touching her communicator while holding up a hand. "One sec."

"Rowena, wide connect."

"As you wish, Lieutenant," Rowena's voice answered in our heads. *"All PPD officers currently connected."*

"Listen up." Rose said. *"This case went from clusterfuck to cataclysmic clusterfuck. Henry is DOD and House Mal is going to be looking for heads, starting with our new chief."*

"Did he kill Henry?" Graffon asked. *"If he did, I'm sure there are statutes that cover the use of excessive force while in PPD custody. Do you need me to brush up on deniability clauses?"*

"I didn't kill Henry," I answered for myself. *"Something called a blood bomb finished him off."*

"Wasn't he already dead?" asked Doe in his monotone way. *"I mean wasn't that the reason he was in The Morgue to begin with? What do you mean a blood bomb finished him off?"*

Rose brought the team up to speed, leaving out the part about my wings and Whoosh.

I let her do it since she knew them longer than I did and I was still establishing a rapport with the team.

Interestingly, there were quite a few curses at the mention of Mage Lowell and The Company.

"What do you need us to do?" Graffon asked.

Rose looked at me and waved for me to answer.

She was letting me take the lead and establishing my position in the group.

I guess saving her ass from instant scorching counted for something. I didn't entirely trust her, the repeated mentions of exploding me and my wings gave me pause, but it seemed like she was warming up to me—probably the same way a dragon warms up to its next meal.

"Graffon," I said, *"you and Doe make the initial approach to The Company. Use the proper channels and inform them that Mage Lowell is being sought as a person of interest in an ongoing investigation."*

"And when they laugh us out of their offices?" Doe asked. *"You realize everyone in The Company is probably being sought for something?"*

"Doesn't matter. The point is to give them a chance to turn the Mage over. When they don't, they'll be obstructing justice."

Rose smiled.

"I like how you think, Chief. Then we go in and blow their HQ to dust!"

"Not exactly," I said as Rose scowled. *"Silk and Butch will*

visit House Mal and speak with Emissary Sinclair. If House Mal is involved, I want to give them the chance to come clean."

"What do you mean 'if'?" Rose said, staring at me.

"You said it yourself, Croft would never work for House Mal, no matter how much they paid him." I gave her a look. *"So, if it wasn't House Mal that actually hired him, then who did?"*

"Sinclair," Rose rasped as we reached the lower level. *"That bastard. But, wait, why would he hire Croft?"*

"Butch and Silk are going to ask him some questions and maybe find out," I replied. *"In the meantime, we're going to have a chat with Nimble and then go see Wind, like you said."*

"You plan on exploding something?" Graffon asked. *"Please let me know what exactly will be the demolished. That way I can prepare the proper position statement regarding the exculpatory clause seven which states that the PPD is not liable ad infinitum as long—"*

"Graffon," I interrupted, heading off a joint brain melting legalese session, *"we get it! Keep your head in the game. When The Company shuts you down, give me a call. Rose and I will start unleashing our deterrents shortly after that. Everyone knows what they need to do?"*

A chorus of *"Got it, Chief,"* was the reply.

"Thanks," I said as I cut off the connector and spoke aloud to Rose. "You didn't have to do that."

"Well, if you plan on sticking around," Rose said as we entered the tech station, "you may as well start acting like a chief. At least that way the bullseye stays on the right back."

"Thanks, I feel all warm and welcomed now," I said, stepping over to the panel next to the large steel door.

"That's what a good lieutenant does. Makes the chief feel all warm and fuzzy."

The last time I'd seen this area, it was to get my tattoo. A goblin by the name of Pecker had done the work via a remote laser system. He wasn't in the Badlands, though. He was seated in Netherworld Proper. I wanted to ask questions, but I'd never had the chance.

I exposed the lines on my arm to the reader attached to the panel and waited.

"A good lieutenant, eh?" I said, mockingly. "When I see one, I'll let you know. Until then I guess I'll have to settle for—"

Rose grabbed me and shoved me back into the stairwell as the lower level exploded.

CHAPTER 20

"*C*hief! Chief! Rose! Anyone?*"

The officers yelling in my head subsided to ear-splitting levels as I opened my eyes and shook off the debris. Rose groaned next to me as she rolled over and kicked off part of the staircase from her legs.

"*We're good,*" Rose said with another groan. "*Minor malfunction down here. You all know how Nimble likes to experiment. Chief gave you assignments, go get them done.*"

Nervous laughter followed as they each signed off. I was about to ask her why she didn't tell them, when she raised a finger.

"*Rowena,*" she said, "*open a secure channel. Authorization Blaze Omega zero-zero-one and two.*"

"*Voice identification verified,*" answered Rowena. Her voice was less AI and more robotic as I heard the switch over in my head. "*Chief Phoenix and Lieutenant Blaze are now on a secure channel with Technician Nimble and the Counter-Terrorist Squad located within the building.*"

"*Thank you, Ro. Monitor and record.*"

"Understood, Lieutenant."

"Nimble?" Rose barked. *"What in the living fuck just happened? Were you trying to blow us up?"*

"It's as I suspected." Nimble answered. *"Can you go over to the panel please?"*

We walked over to the panel where I had revealed my tattoo to the reader.

"There's a hole where the panel used to be," Rose said. *"You're saying it was deliberate?"*

"Who activated the panel? Chief Phoenix?"

"Yes," I said. *"I used the reader just like you showed me."*

"It seems someone would prefer you residing in The Morgue permanently," Nimble replied. *"Are both of you fully intact?"* He didn't wait for a response. *"This smells like Lowell. That little shit, he's using a self-immolating circle keyed to the chief."*

"We're good," Rose said. *"Just a few scratches."* She glanced at me and waved at her face. Scales, she mouthed. *"How are you, Nimble?"*

"Fine."

I looked down and saw my scales had reflexively covered my skin. I focused and retracted them.

"How could he do that?" I asked. *"Wouldn't he need my DNA or something personal?"*

"All he would need is access to the tattoo schematics and then he could integrate the design into the circle and set bombs for you," Nimble replied.

"Doesn't that sound like fun," I said. *"Can you stop him?"*

"It will require some time. The explosion set off failsafes. I'll have to hack the mainframe and reconfigure your tattoo. Rose, if you could—"

"On it," she interrupted. *"I'll send the CTS to get this door opened ASAP."*

"I would really appreciate that, and Chief, don't go anywhere until we redo your ink. I don't know what else may be keyed to explode with you."

The Counter-Terrorist Squad made their way down in less than an hour. They managed to get the door to the tech station open in another twenty minutes.

We stepped into the tech station.

"Ro," Rose said, *"regular communicator channel, please."*

There was a small click and Rowena's snob self returned.

"Request fulfilled, Lieutenant. Will you need anything else?"

"Make sure first responders understand this was just one of Nimble's experiments going sideways," Rose answered. *"No casualties and we'll deal with it down here. Tell them to stay clear until given the go-ahead."*

"Understood."

Nimble was stationed behind a plexan wall partition and facing several banks of computers.

The partition was transparent, several feet in thickness, and it slid into the ceiling as Rose thanked the CTS commander.

Once the area was secure and the tech station was open, they packed up and left the immediate area, leaving a handful of the demolition team to investigate the panel.

I stepped closer and realized they were removing the panel reader from the wall in sections.

Stepping from behind and quickly holstering weapons, were two hellion lab technicians moving around the immediate area. I hadn't seen them when I received my initial tattoo, but that was camera day.

The male was about my height and muscular. He was focused on one of the keyboards near Nimble. The female was shorter and slim. Her eyes held the kind of menace that made Rose look cute and cuddly. She glanced our way and dismissed us as non-threats in the space of half a second.

They moved silently and with quiet purpose. I could tell from the way they held their bodies, they were highly trained.

Beneath their white lab coats, I caught a glimpse of what looked like combat armor.

I glanced over at Rose and motioned to the technicians with my head.

"I don't remember seeing them before." I said, making sure the communicator only connected the two of us. *"New guards?"*

"Those two are Shumants-Shunt Masters and Tactical Security. The male is Yarrl. His partner, the female, is Tam. They come from an obscure house—House Manusht. In addition to being excellent technicians, they are ferocious hellions. Even I would think twice about tangling with them. They keep Nimble and the tech station safe and secure."

"Shunt Masters?"

"Old hellion battlefield martial art designed for maximum devastation and pain."

"Meaning I shouldn't go out of my way to piss them off?"

"Exactly."

There was a commotion at the door and I saw the

demolition team had managed to remove the panels in several sections.

Once it was disassembled, they brought it into the tech station and placed it on a table.

Yarrl moved over to examine it.

I really expected the place to be covered in slime since Nimble was a slug-like creature. Surprisingly, the tech station was clean, bordering on fastidiousness. I didn't know how Nimble managed to keep the slime out of the computers, but I was glad he did.

"Yarrl, prep the machine," Nimble commanded. "We need to re-ink the chief."

"Without Pecker?" Yarrl asked.

"It's just a re-ink," Nimble replied. "The data should already be in place. We'll just need to alter the passcodes and connector access points."

"Standard deviations and adaptations?" Yarrl asked as he arranged the machine. "Any anomalous compensations?"

"Tam, access the chief's file. He *does* have some unique properties we need to compensate for in the ink."

Tam nodded and stepped over to another computer. Her fingers flew over the keys. "Dragon physiology with standard adaptations...hmm," she said and typed again. "We'll need to adjust for this variable, sir."

"Indeed," Nimble said. "He also wields an artifact that allows him to channel a portion of his energy into physical transformation."

"The scales?" Tam said, not looking up from the screen.

"No, look lower," Nimble replied looking at his own

screen. "The artifact bypasses normal neural channels and provides immediate transformation."

"Got it, wings?" Tam asked as she stood and walked over to me. "Adjusted and implemented."

"Be aware of the clearance," Nimble added. "Maintain the integrity of the security level."

Yarrl looked up from his screen. "Director clearance?" he asked. "Is that correct?"

Nimble nodded. "Clearance One, yes."

"Sir?" Tam asked, holding out her hand. "May I borrow your ring? It needs to be scanned."

I handed her Whoosh and she placed it in a scanner that ran a red beam of light over its surface. After a few seconds, Tam checked her screen and nodded handing me back the ring.

"All right, I'm going to do a quick verification check with Pecker," Nimble said. "Hold until I have the go-ahead."

Nimble's appendages flew across the several keyboards in front of him. Usually his definition of speed involved moving slow enough to watch paint dry. That was considered a breakthrough in velocity. Today he was moving really fast, which meant he only moved slowly because he enjoyed pissing everyone off.

"You aren't going to hurt yourself moving that fast?" I asked, amazed at how quickly he was going. "I mean, is something going to go up in flames?"

"Sit over there," Nimble said as he hit a few more keys to prep the machine to redo my tattoo. "Pecker approved the layout." His stalks focused in on me. "Try to sit still. This will only take a few minutes."

"That's what they said last time and it felt much longer than a few minutes."

"Last time Pecker was placing the tattoo for the first time and dealing with your particular physiology," Nimble said quickly. "This time it will be faster since most of the information has been inputted. Plus, last time you were remote."

"What special adaptations were you discussing?" I asked as Yarrl strapped me into the seat and placed the machine over my arm. "Why does it have level one clearance? Even better, what is level one clearance? And did you say Director level one clearance?"

"I'll answer all of your questions the second you're promoted to Director," Nimble replied. "Before that time, all I can say is that it's above all our pay grades. Now hold still. This may hurt—a lot."

CHAPTER 21

The PPD process of inking had many benefits. It unleashed and enhanced abilities PPD officers possessed. In my case, it allowed me to tap into my dragon powers. I could go scaled, and access my wings with or without Whoosh, if I focused enough.

I hadn't tried it yet, but I should've been able to access my full dragon form, in addition to heightened senses and reflexes. For now, I was instructed to remain at half-dragon if I was going to transform.

A half-dragon could beat a full anything in the Badlands. Well, not *anything*, but most things.

I was pretty sure I could take Rose, though. Not that I'd tell her that. She'd probably get upset and then need to prove it by trying to disembowel me or something similar.

Hilda's words came back to me: *A full dragon beats a half anything in the Badlands. Remember that and stop bleeding on my floor, before I really give you something to bleed about.*

I knew better than that. Dragons and hellions were pretty damn even in terms of battling. We had advantages, but so did they.

If dragons were truly that powerful, there'd be no balance in the Badlands.

Without balance, there's only chaos.

Anyway, Hilda wasn't exactly the greatest mother, but valkyries weren't renowned for their parenting skills. They figured if you made it past puberty, their job was done. If you lost your head, or any other limb for that matter—it was your own fault and dying only meant you were too stupid to live.

Nimble started the machine off while Yarrl held it, and me, in place as it redrew and enhanced my ink. I could feel the increased powers and the shift in energy as it removed and then completed the new design. I didn't feel any different, but I *was* curious about the Director-level clearance on my ink.

"I encrypted an evolving design into your ink. Director Clearance allowed for that," Nimble explained. "This should prevent Lowell from keying any future circles to your design."

"The better question is, how did that piece of shit mage get access to the Chief's design in the first place, slug?" Rose said with an undercurrent of menace.

Both Yarrl and Tam looked up at her words. I could sense the subtle shift in their energy and stances. I didn't want to get into it with two Shunt Masters. Whatever that was, it sounded painful.

Nimble appeared unbothered.

He kept his focus on the screen in front of him.

"The same way anyone else would have done it," he answered calmly. "He hacked into the ultra-insecure PPD servers and stole the partial designs."

"Partial designs?" I asked. "He didn't get all of it?"

"No. He couldn't. No one can." Nimble turned the screen my way. "When I say your design has Director Clearance, it means I can only access your design for a short period of time. I could only alter my end. *Your* design came in two parts."

The screen had a counter with thirty seconds remaining on the timer. A large black box covered the space where the design would be seen, with the words 'Director Clearance' in large red letters filling the space. Nimble could execute the design, but he couldn't alter or see the part that was covered.

"And if you take too long?" I asked. "That doesn't look friendly."

"If I extend beyond the allotted time," Nimble answered, hitting some keys and shutting the system down. "My whole system is shut down due to a non-compliant breach and a Director *would* show up here."

"They would come to the Badlands PPD? In person? For a simple design?"

"Director Clearance means there's nothing simple about it," Rose answered. "Your design must contain some serious modifications."

"Have you met the Directors?" Nimble responded, glancing at the still upset Rose. "No thanks. If you feel the need to express your displeasure, Lieutenant, I'm sure Yarrl or Tam would oblige you."

Rose glanced at Tam and gave her a short nod, which was returned.

"I'll take a raincheck on the dance," Rose said. "Nimble, we need to go see Wind."

"Windham?" Nimble asked, swiveling his stalks around to face Rose. "Are you certain?"

Rose nodded. "He may have some insight to an accelerant that was used to try and erase us. Plus, I need to borrow some explosives from him. We need to have a conversation with The Company."

"Borrow?" Nimble replied, tapping on the keys of the keyboard in front of him. "You realize he's a deranged pyromaniac with acute thermobaromania. I advise against spending any time with or near him."

"Thermic barometer?" I asked. "He has hot weather issues?"

"Thermobaromania," Nimble started, "is a condition in which the person enjoys seeing things blown up. A deconstructionist like Windham is dangerous."

I looked over at Rose and could tell her mind was set. "Any precautions we need to take before seeing this 'Wind' person?"

"When you visit him," Nimble started, "don't touch or eat anything. Make sure you know exactly how any device he gives you works. He's been known to give faulty explosives and they've backfired—literally."

"Why would he do that?"

"Did I skip over the thermobaromania regarding his personage?" Nimble asked. "He loves to see things explode. It's a compulsion."

"Wind is going to help us have a conversation with

The Company," Rose answered. "Especially concerning protecting a certain scummy Mage that tried to kill us —twice."

"The Company won't give up Lowell unless you make it painful for them," Nimble replied, tapping some more keys and pointing at the screen. "Here it is. Whoever hacked into the PPD servers did it from this location. I'd assume Lowell is in that vicinity."

I looked over at the screen and heard Rose curse behind me.

"Are you sure?" she asked. "Could your calculations be off?"

One of Nimble's stalks looked away from the screen and focused on Rose.

"Are you questioning my computer skills?" he asked.

The visual of his stalks facing in two different directions was disconcerting at best.

"Well I—" Rose started.

"Do I question if hellions are badasses?" Nimble asked.

I looked over at Yarrl and Tam. My limited exposure to Rose could confirm the badassery of hellions.

"Good point," Rose acquiesced. "I just didn't think Lowell would be there. This is going to be a one-way run."

"One-way run?" I asked. "That doesn't sound promising."

"It's not," Rose answered, her voice grim. "One more thing, slug. We are going to need a diversion. Can you locate the maniac?"

Nimble nodded which made his stalks dance up and down.

"By maniac, I'm assuming you would like Windham's location?"

"As long as it isn't one of the nine levels of Hell, yes," Rose said as Nimble returned to typing. "He's going to provide our introduction."

Nimble pointed to the screen. "According to my sources, a surveillance and transaction trace, Windham is at this location."

Rose leaned in and scowled. "At least it's not Hell."

I looked at the screen.

"Where is that?" I asked. "That looks like the edge of the city."

"It's beyond the edge of the city," Nimble answered. "That property is the estate of Emissary Sinclair a representative of—"

"House Mal?" I finished.

"Precisely," Nimble replied. "Any violence on House property is grounds for prosecution and termination."

Rose was leaving the tech station. "You coming, Chief?"

"What do you mean prosecution and termination?" I asked. "We're PPD."

"On House property, PPD law doesn't apply," Nimble replied. "Think of each House as a small sovereign state or fiefdom. You may be the law in the Badlands—on that estate, in the eyes of the law, you'll just be a trespassing dragon and an angry homicidal hellion."

"Rose," I said, turning around to see she had left. "Shit."

"I'd suggest catching up to her before she dismembers someone."

CHAPTER 22

I caught up to Rose in the garage.

Looking across at the other spaces, I saw my Hurricane silently beckoning to me with a quiet menace. I still didn't know my way around Infernal City well enough to sit behind the wheel yet, though. Yes, it was a grid system, but that didn't mean I wanted to head down the wrong street at the wrong time.

After the day I'd had, it was abundantly clear that my head was on the chopping block.

It made more sense to risk my life with Rose's driving at this point.

Her car roared to life as I strapped in.

"So glad you could make it," she said, screeching out of her parking space and up the ramp. "Let me do the talking at Sinclair's."

"If all you plan on doing is talking, sure," I answered with an edge in my voice that made her glance my way. "Again—and it seriously *does* seem to be the most important aspect of my job so far—let me remind you that we are PPD officers. Don't make me—"

"Not on House property," she shot, back swerving around a column and leaving the PPD garage. "I need Wind, and the moment we step foot in Emissary Sinclair's estate, we aren't PPD. We're a hellion and a dragon looking for a psycho goblin with a hard-on for exploding things."

She probably had a point there.

"And you think Sinclair is just going to hand Wind over to us?"

"I can be very persuasive when I need to be," Rose answered with a smile. "I studied interspecies negotiation in my first year with the PPD. I'm pretty good at it."

"Interspecies negotiation?" I asked in disbelief. "You mean shoot them first and then work out the terms of their surrender?"

"My methods can be...a bit unorthodox," she said, gritting her teeth and shifting gears, cutting off a truck and sliding into oncoming traffic.

She waited for a split second before jumping back into the flow and stepping on the gas.

The Hurricane shot off, leaving the traffic behind.

Great, she was still chief hazing—the joy.

"Seriously," I said, "how do you intend to get Wind to cooperate with us?"

"One second," she replied, placing a hand to her communicator. *"Ro, put us wide."*

"Officer chat enabled, Lieutenant," Rowena answered.

"Listen up," Rose started. *"The Chief and I are headed over*

to Sinclair's. Butch, once you and Silk are done with House Mal, swing on by to our location, copy?"

"Emissary Sinclair's?" Butch answered. *"That's hellion territory."*

"Thanks Butch," Rose scoffed. *"I know where it is. Just make sure you don't violate any of the codes of conduct when you visit House Mal."*

"You mean the same codes you're about to break the moment you set foot on Sinclair's property?" Silk's voice chimed in. *"Let me guess, you're going to use your infamous negotiation skills?"*

Laughter erupted over the communicator. Rose scowled and I couldn't help but crack a smile, making sure she didn't see it.

At least it wasn't only *me* being made fun of. That was something. Not much, but something.

Maybe I would get along with this crew, after all.

Still, I wasn't about to let her wallow in getting ribbed. I needed to show some chiefatude here.

"You're acting officers of the PPD," I said with moderate sternness. *"I expect you all to conduct yourselves as lawfully as possible"*—I remembered Croft in The Morgue—*"until you no longer have the option. Then we uphold the law of the Badlands."*

"Damn straight," Rose finished by closing the channel. "Kill or be killed. You may just make it to the end of the week, Chief."

"Your confidence in my life expectancy is incredibly encouraging," I said, gripping the door as she managed to go even faster. "At least the duration lengthens slightly with each of your comments."

"Does it?" she replied, as if fishing around in her thoughts.

And that's when we saw the flames.

Either something was wrong or Emissary Sinclair was holding the largest barbecue in the Badlands.

"Fuck," Rose growled as she swerved onto the road that led to the estate. "This smells like The Company."

That would mean that the rest of my squad was going to be showing up to a real barn burner.

"Do we need to warn Graffon and Doe?" I asked.

"Graffon is a Demonoid, and Doe is a Faceless," Rose smiled at some secret thought. "We should probably warn The Company."

We pulled up to the front of the estate, Rose kept the Hurricane a good distance from the blaze as we got out.

"Ro, we need fire control out here at the Emissary's estate," I heard Rose say in my head as we approached the main house. *"Someone decided Sinclair was no longer useful and torched his place. Probably with him in it."*

"Did the Chief start the fire?" Rowena asked.

"What the—?" I glanced at Rose.

Her smirk was so deep it looked like a tattoo.

"No," Rose answered, *"we just arrived on scene and the blaze was going when we got here. We're going to confirm if Sinclair is inside. Get Fire Control down here now, and call Francis at The Morgue. A house this large has staff."*

"Had staff," Rowena argued. *"Fire Control is on its way."*

"Excellent," Rose answered, stopping at the entrance. *"I'll give you a sitrep after the Chief determines if there are any survivors."*

I was glancing around at the flames when the weight of Rose's words hit me.

"What do you mean after *I* determine if there are any survivors?" I asked, staying back from the flames licking at the window frames. "Why aren't we waiting for Fire Control?"

Rose stepped a little further away from the intense heat and crossed her arms.

"Because time is of the essence," she said, her jaw set. "This is The Company tying up loose ends and stinks like that scum piece of shit mage, Lowell. I doubt Sinclair made it out of this unscorched, but fire and explosions are Wind's specialty. There's a good chance he's still alive in there somewhere. Besides, you're the dragon. Flame is kind of your thing, remember?"

"Not really, no."

"Sure it is," Rose said, encouragingly. "We never did get to test the rocket launcher, but this is the next best thing." She nodded and pointed at me. "Yes, think of it as a field test."

"A...huh?"

"Don't worry," she said, studying the area, "I'll be right here, away from the intense fire, monitoring the situation."

I looked at the raging flames.

As a dragon, I could appreciate the inherent destructive beauty. As Chief of the Badlands PPD, though, I didn't enjoy the thought of running into a blazing inferno.

"This is going to suck," I grumbled as I channeled

energy into my body forcing my scales to form. "Let's do this!"

I pressed Whoosh, formed my wings, and half-ran, half-glided into the blaze.

CHAPTER 23

*R*unning into a fire is not my idea of a warm reception. I used my wings to form a flame resistant perimeter around my body as I looked around the interior. My scales gave off a red glow as the heat increased around me. To be honest, I wasn't feeling uncomfortable—*yet.*

I'd never tested the heat tolerances of my dragon form.

The valkyries who raised me focused more on my fighting ability than my dragon self. I knew I could take heat and flames, but maybe Rose was right. Having an accurate assessment of what my limits were would be good information to obtain.

The only problem with that idea was her execution of the data gathering. I had a feeling it involved strapping high explosives to different parts of my body.

I shook my head to focus on the task at hand —survivors, if there were any.

I let my senses expand and was immediately hit with

an onslaught of smells and sounds. I dialed it back and tried to filter the smells as I moved from room to room.

From the looks of things, the fire started in several places. I wasn't an arson investigator, but I could tell there were several origin points. The charred bodies of the staff were good clues too. It seemed like Lowell had rigged the employees of the estate to explode simultaneously throughout the house. This was Henry all over again, except no blood imps.

Hopefully.

Part of me was glad they went fast and felt no pain, but I'd make sure that piece of shit mage would suffer long and hard for this.

I ran throughout the ground floor realizing that the fire was intensifying. I was racing against time and the fire. Any moment now, the structural integrity of the house would fail and parts of the upper levels would come crashing down.

I found Sinclair, or what was left of him in the kitchen.

He had burst into flame and exploded into hellion parts all over the center island of the large space. I noticed the residue of a circle etched into the marble counter opposite where the bottom half of Sinclair stood. He never had a chance. I almost felt sorry for the pompous ass, but my dragon nature kicked in and empathy left the building.

I stood still for a second and listened.

There was a heartbeat, but it was distant. How anyone could be alive in this inferno astounded me. I was beginning to feel the heat and knew I had to get out of here soon.

If Wind was alive, it wasn't on this level.

"Rose," I said through the connector, *"Sinclair is dust—literally. I don't see Wind anywhere, but I hear a heartbeat. Any suggestions where he would be in this place?"* There wasn't an immediate response. *"Running out of time, Rose,"* I pressed. *"This place is going to come down any second."*

"Any sane person would try and find someplace safe," Rose's voice came over a second later. *"Wind, however, is a pyro. He'd go where he could experience the full effect of the flames."*

"How could he do that?" I asked. *"I mean without being a dragon?"*

"Use your dragon senses and find him—fast. I hear Fire Control sirens."

"Shit, on it."

I shut out the world as much as possible and listened. I filtered out the ambient noises, the sound of the fire devouring everything in its path, the creaking wood, and shattering glass.

That's when I singled it out from everything else.

It was definitely a heart beating.

Fast.

Upstairs.

Upstairs made no sense, though.

Everyone knows that's the worst place to go if you're trapped in a fire. I ran up the main staircase using the heat from the flames to give my wings lift. They were too large to fully extend indoors, but they gave me a boost getting to the second floor landing.

I pulled them close to my body and ran from room to room, doing my best to follow the heartbeat. Down a corridor to the last room on the left. I kicked in the door and jumped in.

Standing in the center of the room, with a lighter in his hand stood a small figure in protective clothing. The figure whirled on me as soon as I opened the door.

"You stupid idiot!" screamed a voice. "Get out!"

A ball of flame blossomed in the center of the room around the figure. I grabbed him and ran across the floor to the windows, crashing through them into the cool air. An explosion rocked the main house, destroying the second level.

I landed near Rose and the Hurricane. The figure wriggled out of my arms and kicked me in the shin.

Had I not been scaled I might've felt it.

"You're welcome, you little shit," I hissed, dodging another kick.

"Wind," Rose said calmly.

"Did it look like I needed a rescue?" Wind yelled. "I had a perfect backdraft setup. The room was primed!"

"Wind," Rose said again.

"And who comes crashing in?" Wind gestured at me. "Captain Clueless here." The glare was nearly as hot as the flames. "Who the hell are you anyway?"

"Wind," Rose said again, with an edge. "I need your attent—"

"Do you know how hard it is to get a primed backdraft?" Wind continued, ignoring Rose. I stepped back when I saw her face. "True, that freak Lowell almost cooked me, but it was worth it. It was a perfect—"

Rose backhanded the goblin over the Hurricane.

He landed with a thud and a groan.

"Damn, Rose," Wind said, getting to his feet. "If you want to talk, why don't you just say so? No need to get physical...unless you really want to?"

Wind waggled his eyebrows and Rose drew one of her guns. Wind ran behind the Hurricane again.

"Stick that ugly head out, I'll show you physical," Rose said taking aim. "I don't need much, Wind. Just the tip will do just fine."

"That's what she said," Wind shot back and leapt to the side as Rose fired several rounds in his direction, hitting the car.

The Hurricane was unscathed and I got the impression she wasn't really trying to shoot him, at least not anywhere lethal.

The Fire Control sirens were getting closer.

"We need him mostly alive," I said, grabbing Wind by the shoulder as he tried to scamper away from the approaching Rose. "You can shoot him after he helps us."

"Help you?" Wind asked, looking up at me. "Who the hell *are* you?"

Rose clamped Wind by the throat focusing his attention.

"Right now," Rose whispered. "I'm in a bad mood that's getting worse. I need *you* to rig the Oasis to blow."

Wind's eyes focused at the word *blow*. He pointed at his neck and Rose loosened her grip.

"The Oasis is the largest Company-owned casino on the Strip," Wind started with an expression approximating glee. "Is this a real deal or are we just dry humping here? Don't jerk me around, Rose." He looked up and pursed his lips. "Actually, I wouldn't mind that either, in a literal sense anyway."

"The Company is protecting Lowell," Rose replied, still holding his neck. "I need to ask the mage some questions."

"You're using the Oasis as a conversation starter?" Wind asked, wiping the drool from the corner of his mouth. "I love how your twisted mind works."

"Wait a second," I chimed in. "No one said anything about blowing up a casino. Not only are there going to be some pretty pissed off shareholders, those places are filled with customers, remember?"

"Not after a fire drill," Wind answered. "They clear the premises for an hour while the drill is executed."

Rose nodded at me as if to say 'Get it? Got it? Good!'

She then turned back to Wind, smiling the smile of devastation.

"Can you do it, or is this job too big for you?"

"Leon will shit his pants if something happens to the Oasis," Wind muttered. "No one dares touch a Company property."

"Call me a daredevil," Rose replied, letting Wind go. "Yes or no?"

I drew Butterfly.

"You're not blowing up anything if it's going to involve innocent bystanders," I said, aiming at Wind. "There'd better be a plan B."

Wind looked at Rose and raised an eyebrow.

"Listen, tall, dark, and spooky," the goblin said, stepping close as Rose released her grip. "This is the Badlands. No such thing as innocent *anything* in this town."

"How long?" Rose asked, pushing Butterfly to the side. "I need a window."

"I can use my connection in Fire Control to call in a drill," Wind said, rubbing his chin. "Then, I'll set the implosion charges *during* the drill." He looked up at her. "Are we bringing down the whole place or is this window dressing?"

"I'm insane," Rose said, "but I'm not *that* insane. We destroy the Oasis, we start a war."

"No war-starting, thank you," I said, quickly. "Definitely a 'no' on going to war with The Company, and anyone for that matter."

"You take out the Oasis," Wind said quietly, "you'll get Master's attention. That's attention you don't need."

"Non-essential property implosion," Rose answered. "They're going to call my bluff and I need to make them reconsider their priorities. Like how attached they may be to life."

Wind's face fell for a moment and then lit up again. "Can I rig the garage and take out their vehicles?" A hopeful goblin was even stranger looking than a non-hopeful one. "That's pretty non-essential." He batted his eyelashes. "Say 'yes' please? If I can get the garage, I can be ready inside of three hours."

"Like the chief said," Rose said, nodding and thumbing a finger back at me, "no innocent bystanders are to be hurt."

"Chief?" Wind asked, giving me the once over. "Chief of what?"

"Badlands PPD," I said, giving him my fiercest dragon stare. "Don't mess this up."

Wind took a step back, staring at me. "Rose, your chief looks like he needs to take a dump."

"No casualties," Rose said, opening the door to the Hurricane, "or I'm going to stick an explosive so far up your—"

"Promise?" he interrupted, clearly knowing where she was going with that threat. "I love when you use that sexy hellion talk. I'll give you a call. Three hours."

He ran off as Rose started the car and pulled away while the Fire Control trucks started arriving on the scene. She rolled down a window and flashed her badge to the lead firefighter.

He stopped barking orders for a second.

"I need a report of any findings when you're done," Rose said, looking at his badge. "Lieutenant Fand."

"Sorry, Lieutenant," the firefighter answered. "You need to go through Arson Investigation. If there's something suspicious you can have your chief make a request."

Rose flexed her jaw and tightened her grip on the steering wheel

Fand was blowing her off.

This was one of those interdepartmental pissing contests. The only problem being that Lieutenant Fand didn't know how close he was to losing the ability to piss without assistance ever again.

"I'm making the request now," I said from my seat, showing my badge. "Have the report on her desk by the morning, Lieutenant."

Lieutenant Fand jumped when he heard my voice and

I saw the look of shock settle into his face as he examined my badge.

"Yes, sir," he answered, quickly. "I mean yes, Chief, Sir."

Rose smiled, rolled up the window, and gunned the engine, screeching away from the scene.

"I was just about to use my negotiating skills on him," Rose said flying down the road.

"That's what I was afraid of."

CHAPTER 24

"Three hours," Rose said. "You need to brief the team." She touched her communicator. *"Ro, wide please."*

"Officer chat enabled, Lieutenant," Rowena answered.

"Chief has some instructions, listen up." Rose said, without looking at me.

"Silk and Butch, swing by the Sinclair estate and see what you can glean," I commanded, feeling like I was at least partially getting the hang of things. Like it or not, Rose *was* educating me. Not in the way I would have preferred, but it was effective nonetheless. *"Lowell cast immolation circles on the staff and around the property. It was nasty work. Everyone's goal is to learn what Fire Control uncovers."*

"That Lowell is a sick son-of-a-bitch," Butch said.

"What did House Mal say?" I asked, not expecting much. *"Did they sanction Sinclair's actions?"*

"Yeah," Butch started. *"The, uh, representative here says Sinclair has been off the reservation for—"* I heard the rustle

of paper "—*about six months. They were going to have him relieved of duty. Guess The Company took care of that.*"

I nodded before remembering this was a connector conversation. "*We're on our way to The Company,*" I said. "*Graffon, any progress?*"

"*If, by progress, you mean having several dozen weapons pulled on us after we informed them Lowell was wanted for questioning, then yes we've made tremendous progress.*"

"*They'll give him up,*" Rose said. "*Head back to HQ and gear up, things are going to get dicey in a few hours.*"

"*All our gear is in the car,*" Graffon answered. "*It was more efficient to carry it with us since our new chief is a dragon and, statistically speaking, dragons have been known to wreak havoc in eighty percent of their encounters with the general populace.*" She paused. "*As a matter of fact, in the other twenty percent they were indirect catalysts for mayhem and destruction.*"

"*Graffon?*" Rose asked.

"*Yes, would you like me to break down the analysis by cross-sectional data and varying demographics?*" Graffon answered. "*If you have time, I could even demonstrate the increased potential for fatalities as a result of having a dragon chief. It's quite fascinating.*"

"*No, thank you Graffon,*" I said, rubbing my temples. "*Why not save that for later? I'm sure Rose would love to hear all about it over a pot of coffee and a couple of donuts.*"

"*Will do, Chief!*" Graffon responded excitedly as Rose shot me a dark look.

"*Our gear is in the car too,*" Silk piped up, "*but only because Butch hates changing in the PPD locker room. Last time someone made fun of Malkyries, he broke that idiot's legs in three places."*

"It was an accident," Butch defended himself. *"Sometimes I don't know my own strength."*

I shook my head as Rose grinned.

This was going to take some getting used to.

"Graffon and Doe, pull back," I said. *"I don't want you in the middle of a firefight before we have a conversation with The Company."*

"By conversation," Doe asked, his voice deadpan, *"do you mean things exploding, death, and destruction? I ask because that sounds like one of the lieutenant's conversations."*

"Something like that," I answered, glancing over at Rose. *"We really need to apprehend and prosecute Mage Lowell."*

"Apprehend and prosecute," Silk chimed in with a chuckle. *"So that's what we're calling it now?"*

"When I say 'apprehend and prosecute,' I mean apprehend and prosecute," I stated firmly. *"I do not mean 'shoot dead and throw their body on the Strip as a cautionary tale.' Am I clear?"*

"Sure, Chief," they all chimed in as Rose glanced at me and shrugged. *"We understand."*

"Where are we headed?" I asked, noticing the rising tension in Rose's grip on the steering wheel, as I shut down the connector.

"We need to give Wind time to get set up," Rose answered. "I'm going to try and find out why they have such a hard-on for our new chief."

"And we need to get there in a hurry?" I asked, noticing the digits climbing steadily on the digital display speedometer. Then I glanced out the back window. "Maybe someone is chasing us?"

"Someone wants you dead," Rose answered, her voice on edge. "Enough to kill a hellion diplomat and emissary. Killing dragons is one thing. Killing hellions because of a dragon? That pisses me off."

"How about we avoid the whole killing thing entirely?" I asked.

"Then this wouldn't be the Badlands, Chief," Rose answered, pulling off onto a deserted road. "We're going to speak to someone who would know why."

CHAPTER 25

"*W*ho are we going to see?" I asked, looking around and realizing we were in the middle of nowhere. "Who would live out here?"

"Pytha lives out here." Rose answered and touched her communicator. "*Ro, we need to go off grid.*"

"*Authorization please, Lieutenant,*" Rowena answered inside my head.

"*Authorization zero-zero-one and two,*" Rose replied. "*Initiate Ghost Protocol.*"

"*Please be aware, the rest of the officers will only be able to track to your last known position,*" Rowena answered. "*Until Ghost Protocol is disengaged, you will not be able to call for assistance and communication will be limited to you and the Chief. Do you comply with these terms, Lieutenant?*"

"Understood," Rose said. "*Initiate the protocol.*"

"*Voice authorization confirmed,*" Rowena answered. "*Ghost Protocol initiated, be safe.*"

"I never do safe, Ro," Rose said with a smile. "*Did you get that?*"

"Ghost Protocol?" I asked. "And what did you mean about being off the grid?"

"Exactly what it sounds like," Rose answered. "The communicators are excellent for coordinating with and speaking to the team. They're also a perfect way of keeping tabs on us and our locations."

"So we're not really off-grid?"

"Only chiefs and lieutenants can access Ghost Protocol," Rose replied, slowing down and switching onto another less traveled road. We meandered through thicker forest at this point. The trees overhead lending an ominous feel to the place. "Sometimes Badlands PPD officers need to engage in activity that can't be tracked or reported—like now."

"Is it like this for other PPD precincts?"

She gave me a shocked look. "How the fuck do I know?"

I grimaced at her.

"Can Nimble track us?" I asked, realizing how something like this protocol could be abused. "Or is he in the dark, too?"

"Rowena diverts all Ghost Protocol activity to a special server," Rose answered. "Access to that server requires unanimous consent from all the Directors, along with biometric compliance—fingerprint and iris scan."

"Then Nimble knows we've gone dark," I said. "Just not *where* we're going after our last drop point."

"That's all he knows," Rose answered. "Only Directors know the location of the server. Nimble gets an alert of our last known position in case of an emergency or if he needs to mobilize the other officers."

"And everyone has to give consent? I asked. "Can't imagine that would be easy to obtain." I noticed the house at the end of the road. Rose stopped the car a good distance from the entrance. "Why are we stopping here?"

"Because I enjoy breathing," Rose said, quietly. "Get out and don't make any sudden moves. Pytha is obsessive about her privacy."

We stepped out of the car and I looked around. Nothing seemed out of the ordinary, but those were the scenarios where I had to be the most careful.

I remembered my training days.

When things seemed the calmest is when I had to worry.

Hilda's voice came back to me: *Appear weak when you are strong and strong when you are weak. This is our way. If that fails, a blade through the throat usually stops most attacks. This is also our way.*

Several drones hovered to our location. They remained a good distance away from us, but I could see the cameras attached to their bodies. Some of them were equipped with what appeared to be small missiles. Others appeared to be outfitted with guns. Another small group of them clustered behind us and remained hovering out of reach.

Rose looked up.

"It's me," Rose said. "We need to talk."

"What took you so long?" an elderly voice answered from the center drone. "I was expecting you days ago."

"We've been busy," Rose said, glancing my way. "Plus, I didn't know if I could trust him."

"He's a dragon," the voice said with a small chuckle. "Can you ever really trust a dragon?"

"I'm the Badlands PPD Chief," I retaliated. "Of course you can—"

"I know who you are, boy," the voice cut me off. "Make sure you both mind the path. I'm not cleaning up bits of you because you were stupid."

"She sounds pleasant," I said under my breath. "Who is she again?"

"Communicators, Chief," Rose's voice whispered in my head. *"Keep your comments and opinions to yourself. I'm not in the mood to die today."*

CHAPTER 26

ose led the way to the small house. All along, the drones hovered nearby, ready to remind us of the lethal stupidity of veering off the path.

"Who needs this much security?" I asked, glancing at the drones floating around us like some kind of mutant insects. "I mean really? She's in the middle of nowhere."

"There's a reason she's in the middle of nowhere," Rose answered. "Follow me and don't step off the path."

"What path?" I said, looking down.

"The one that will keep you alive as we get closer to the house," she pointed down. "The little glittery bits. Pay attention."

I followed her arm and realized there *was* a stone path, which you could only see if you noted the glittery bits. It made me wonder how many people had fallen to the drones over the years due to nearsightedness.

That made me think that there may be other reasons for the drones to attack. I released my dragon senses, slightly. I didn't know if the freaky things would react to spikes in power, and I didn't want to take a chance in getting us shredded by accident.

Besides, I had a feeling a drone attack wouldn't put Rose in a good mood. Not that she ever approximated having a pleasant mood unless death, mayhem, and destruction were involved.

My senses were still engaged enough to pick up on the net of energy surrounding the property.

That meant the drones were actually the least of our worries.

All around the house, extending for several hundred feet in every direction, were a series of failsafes, traps, and energy neutralizers.

No one was storming Pytha's home anytime soon.

"Who is this person again?" I asked as we stood in front of the door after navigating her 'yard of death'.

"If you have anything questionable to say," Rose said, tapping her temple. "Make sure you keep it personal."

I understood what she meant.

Rose leaned in to the door. A beam of blue light scanned her face horizontally and then vertically.

"Facial recog?" I asked using my communicator. *"Is this some emissary from another House?"*

"Something like that," Rose replied in my head. *"We don't have much time. We ask our questions and get the hell out."*

The facial scan finished processing Rose's face. I assumed she was cleared since the door clicked open a few seconds later. The drones behind us hovered off and disappeared into the trees.

Somehow, that didn't make me feel any safer.

Rose stepped inside and motioned for me to follow.

We walked into a small foyer. I noticed a staircase leading up. To our right a large door led to a sitting room. Ahead of us and past the foyer, French doors opened to what I imagined was a sunroom, judging from the light.

The entire space felt warm and lived in.

"You took your time getting here," the same elderly voice from the drone said behind us. "What's so damn urgent that you felt the need to drag me away from my afternoon tea?"

We turned and looked down at an older woman. This was not the frail elderly type. She looked fit enough to take on both of us for an afternoon workout session. Dark glasses covered her eyes. Her light beige dress contained red accents and flowed around her as she glided gracefully to the French doors.

There was something familiar about her, but I couldn't place the sensation. Her long black hair was streaked with white as she walked on ahead of us.

"Pytha," Rose began, "this is our new chief, Zeke Phoenix."

"Ezekias," I said holding out a hand. "A pleasure."

"We'll see about that," Pytha answered, pulling down her glasses and glancing up at me. She looked down at my hand before turning around and stepping through the doors. "Come on in, may as well get this over with. I'm sure there are people to kill somewhere."

I stood there in shock as the realization hit me. Her eyes told me everything I needed to know.

"Why didn't you tell me?" I asked Rose.

"Would you have believed me, if I had?" Rose answered. *"Let's do this. She's not known for being the patient type."*

"You could've at least told me."

"You don't understand the risk I'm taking just being here," Rose snapped. *"Much less being here with you. Telling you would have accomplished nothing. A handful of people know of this location. That's for their safety as much as it is for Pytha. Let's go."*

Rose was right. I didn't know what role Pytha played in the dynamics of the Badlands. Whatever she did, it was risky, especially if she was speaking to the Badlands PPD. This explained the insane amounts of security. If anyone found out about her, or where she lived, she'd be at the top of every assassin's to-do list.

It had hit me when she revealed her eyes.

Pytha was a dragon.

CHAPTER 27

*P*ytha sat in a large chair in the sunroom and crossed her legs, looking at me.

"Someone is trying to kill the chief," Rose started. "I mean at first I thought—"

"He's the chief," Pytha interrupted with a shrug. "It's a common thing for everyone to try and kill the new chief, right?"

"Sure," Rose said, rubbing her chin. "And, normally, I wouldn't give a shit. No offense, Chief."

Rose was just warm feelings all over, similar to the sensation of how blood covered you after a gunshot wound to the chest.

"None taken," I muttered, still looking at Pytha. "I mean, no more than the usual."

"You came all this way to tell me your chief was in danger?" Pytha asked with an edge to her voice. "Tell me this is *not* the reason you are wasting my time."

"Two hellions are dead because of him," Rose pointed at me. "I thought the first one, a diplomat, was part of a funeral party. I was mistaken. The second was Emissary Sinclair, who is probably still warm. At least what's left of him. If this keeps up we're headed for—"

"War," Pytha removed her glasses and stared at me. "What House do you belong to, dragon?"

"I'm not sure I understand the question," I said. "I was raised by valkyries. They don't really have Houses, more like clans. My mother, rather the woman who raised me, is named Hilda."

"The Terror?" Pytha asked, surprise tinging her response. "Well, that would explain why you're still alive. You can probably fight."

"He can," Rose said. "Doesn't explain why they're coming after him more than usual, though. This isn't just some kill-the-new-chief sort of thing, Pytha. This is...more."

Pytha stared at Rose for a few seconds. Then she motioned at me. "Let me see your markings, dragon."

I stepped up to her and showed her my arm. Her grip was reminiscent of a vise trying to squeeze my arm flat. She examined the tattoos on my forearm, shook her head, and smiled.

"Clever," she said after a moment. "Your PPD ink covers your markings, making them impossible to decipher."

"Was that done intentionally?" Rose asked, looking at her own tattoos.

"That'd be my guess," Pytha replied, still gripping my arm and cutting off the flow of blood. "Look at where his ink is placed. Higher and centered. Exactly where dragon House markings would be."

"That means someone in the PPD knows what House he's in and has tried to cover it up," Rose said, narrowing her eyes at my tattoo. "Why would they do that?"

"They didn't *try* to cover it up," Pytha said. "They damn well *succeeded* by using obscuring ink, and also what looks like a recently-added evolving pattern." She squeezed my arm more firmly. "Show me your scales."

"My scales?"

"Did I stutter?" Pytha asked. "Or can you not get them up?"

"Excuse me?" I replied, fidgeting slightly. "I *do not* have an issue with my scales, thank you very much."

"I hear it's a common problem with male dragons," Pytha said with a grin, gripping even harder. "Scales—if you can?"

I focused my anger and let my scales appear. They formed all over my body except the arm where Pytha had me gripped. I tapped into more dragon energy and her hand flew off my arm as if yanked away.

I was gasping at the exertion, which was something that had never happened before.

"How did you do that?" I asked, catching my breath. "How did you stop my scales?"

"I'm a dragon and I'm old," Pytha replied, still peering at my arm. "The ink used by the PPD compensated for the scales. Someone did their homework." She peered up at me. "Want my advice?"

My initial reaction was to say that the only reason we came out here, in the middle of nowhere, was for her help. That should've been obvious, but I had a feeling she would've used that iron grip of hers to rip off my arm and beat me senseless with it.

I was learning.

Instead, I said, "Yes, please."

"Go have a conversation with Hilda," Pytha said. "I'm sure she knows more than she has let on."

"A conversation?" I asked, blinking. "With Hilda?"

"Probably your best course of action," Pytha replied. "That is if you survive all the violence you're about to embark on."

Pytha didn't know what she was asking. A conversation with Hilda started with the point of a blade and usually ended with that point being buried in your midsection.

I'd rather face The Company.

"You can't help us at all?" Rose asked, clearly expecting that Pytha would have held the key to this lock. "I mean... do you have *any* idea who would want a dragon chief dead this badly?"

Pytha gave us a short laugh.

"Dragons aren't exactly loved, girl," she replied with a shake of her head. She stood up slowly and stared at me. "I can tell you one thing, whatever is going on here runs deep. Deep in the PPD and deep in your friends, The Company."

"We aren't friends with The Company," I answered.

"Today's enemy is tomorrow's friend," Pytha said, moving back to the foyer with us in tow. "Don't discount the usefulness of an entity like The Company. Look at hellions and dragons, we each keep the other in check, establishing balance."

"The Company tried to kill us a few times already."

"And haven't succeeded—yet," Pytha said with a nod of admiration. "I'd say you're doing well. It's quite possible the PPD will be the check and balance to The Company, something they are trying to prevent."

"We need to face Mage Lowell," Rose said, as if a lightbulb flipped on at Pytha's words.

"Ah, now I understand," Pytha said, reaching into the pocket of her dress and handed Rose a small vial. "Why didn't you say so, girl? Are you going to kill Lowell this time?"

The vial was about two inches long and filled with a dark liquid. Orange energy raced around the inside of the vial as Rose pocketed it out of sight.

"That's the plan," Rose said. "I should have done this long ago."

"It wasn't the right time long ago," Pytha replied with a wave of her hand. The front door clicked open. "I'm sorry I can't help you any more than that. Remember to stay on the path as you leave the property. It'd be a real shame if you exploded on your way out."

"Thank you," I said. "Any help you've given us is appreciated, though I honestly don't know if you gave us any or not."

"Don't thank me just yet," Pytha replied. "If she drinks that vial, you may very well have to kill her right after Mage Lowell."

Rose headed off down the path with a nod and a wave.

"What's in that vial?" I asked Pytha, watching as Rose padded away. "Why would you give it to her if it's that dangerous?"

"Two things," Pytha said, holding up her index and middle finger. She looked into my eyes and I could sense the undercurrent of energy coming off her. This was a dangerous dragon. "First, you never get to question my motives—ever."

"I apologize, I just meant—" I started.

She curled her index finger. "And two, you are a fucking dragon. Start acting like one or I'll hunt you down myself and put you out of your misery."

"Thank you," I muttered as I turned to follow the path back to the car. "I'll keep that in mind."

"You do that," Pytha said with a smile and a wave. "Have fun fighting The Company. Try not to get dead."

"hat's in the vial?" I asked as the engine roar settled into a purr and we pulled away from Pytha's Den of Destruction.

"Insurance," Rose said, her voice hard. "I don't want to use it, but if it comes to that, you may have to put me down like Pytha said."

"No way," I said, immediately. "You're an officer of the PPD, not some feral animal to be put down. We'll figure out another way to—"

"Once I take that vial, all of you are in danger," Rose interrupted. "I don't mind tearing you to pieces. You're a dragon after all. You kind of have it coming. But I won't harm my fellow officers."

"Thanks for caring," I remarked. "Now, what's in the vial?"

"You *won't* let me hurt them, Chief," Rose replied, looking straight ahead with her jaw flexed as we sped down the road. It wasn't a request. "Are we clear?"

"Completely," I said, having no intention of killing my

lieutenant. "If you tell me what's in the vial, maybe Nimble can reverse engineer—"

"*Ro,*" Rose said, ignoring my suggestion. "*Disengage Ghost Protocol. Authorization Blaze Alpha zero-zero-one and two.*"

"*Ghost Protocol disengaged,*" Rowena answered. "*Welcome back Lieutenant.*"

"*Open a wide channel,*" Rose said. "*We need to check in with the team and I need the whereabouts of Wind.*"

"*Right away Lieutenant, good to see you back safe and sound,*" Rowena answered. "*Team chat available.*"

"*The Chief is here too, Ro,*" Rose said.

"*I noticed,*" Rowena answered coldly. "*Would you like an update on the current status of the team, Lieutenant?*"

"*Yes, I would,*" I cut in. "*Considering* I'm *the chief and I'm the one responsible for them.*"

"*Very well, Chief,*" Rowena said, suddenly pleasant.

There was some cursing and laughter from the officers. The loudest cursing came from Rose beside me.

"Fuck," she said under her breath banging on the steering wheel. "You couldn't wait one more day? I just lost five hundred."

"*That's five hundred owed to me, Lieutenant,*" Graffon said over the communicator. "*I correctly estimated when the chief would, as you said, 'grow a pair' and put Rowena in her place.*"

"*We should've never gone up against Graffon,*" Silk said with a laugh. "*Demons are just plain scary.*"

"*Technically,*" Graffon answered. "*I'm half-demon. My other half, which is Void—*"

"*No one cares, Graffon,*" a chorus of the officers responded.

"It did *take him forever to grow a pair though,"* Silk said, chuckling.

"Yeah, no kidding," Butch responded. *"Big dragon being pushed around by an A.I. So embarrassing."*

"Have you seen your outfit today?" Silk asked. *"Being seen with you in public. That's what's embarrassing."*

"There's nothing wrong with my outfit," Butch shot back. *"You're just jealous."*

So I was the butt of the joke. Not surprising, actually, and it was probably a good thing. If they rallied as a team because of me, fine.

"In any case, I have won the AI Chief pool," Graffon announced. *"As anticipated, the propensity for the new chief to temporarily align himself with the status quo has a predictable and measurable—"*

"You won, Graffon," Rose cut in with a groan. *"No need to torture us."*

"Status reports," I said, enjoying the levity of the moment. Again, I didn't mind being the focus of the current hazing-the-chief pool. I knew it came with the position. If it bonded the team, then so much the better. *"Let me have the sitreps. Graffon?"*

"We are currently positioned several blocks away from the Tower, also known as Company HQ and awaiting further instructions."

"Butch and Silk," I asked, *"any new developments at the Emissary's estate?"*

"I don't know what you did to Lieutenant Fand," Silk said, *"but he's been super cooperative. Even gave us the preliminary report on the cause of the fire. Oh, and by the way, Emissary Sinclair is dead."*

"We kind of figured that," Rose said. *"What did the report say about the cause of the fire?"*

"Inconclusive," Silk replied. I felt certain that I heard the sound of papers rustling. *"Several instances of spontaneous combustion, which led to the formation of a conflagration. Said conflagration caused the structural integrity of the domicile of one Emissary Sinclair Mal to fail, which resulted in the demise of all the inhabitants within the premises—ugh I sound like Graffon now. I need to go wash my mouth out."*

"Inconclusive my ass," Rose hissed. *"That was The Company and Mage Lowell cleaning house—literally."*

"Silk and Butch," I said, *"meet up with Graffon and sit tight. We are going to speak to The Company and convince them to hand over Lowell."*

"This should be great," Silk said. *"Who's doing the talking?"*

"We're going to start with Rose and then—"

"Fucking awesome," Silk said. *"That means bodies and explosions everywhere. Unleash the badassery!"*

I glanced over at Rose who shrugged.

"What can I say?" she said, pulling onto the Strip. "Hellions *are* badass."

CHAPTER 29

*W*e sped down the Strip. In the distance, I saw The Tower. It was one of the tallest buildings in Infernal City. A black gleaming monolith, standing over and looking down at, the rest of the Strip. A testament to The Company's power and corruption.

"Ro," Rose said, *"give me Wind's twenty and patch me into his phone."*

"According to his phone, Windham is currently on the premises of the Oasis," Rowena answered. *"It is presently undergoing a fire drill test."*

"That little bastard actually managed to get it done," Rose said, surprised. *"Get him on the line."*

"Connecting now," Rowena answered.

"Shit, Rose, you nearly just vaporized most of the Oasis with this call," Wind answered with a chuckle. *"What the fuck do you want? I'm handling several hundred pounds of high explosives and inserting blaster caps."*

"Are you ready yet?"

"What the hell do you think I'm doing down here, playing with myself?"

"The way you feel about explosions?" Rose answered. "It's definitely a possibility. We're on our way to see Leon. I need those explosives in place or we are never going to leave that office—alive."

"The parking garage is done," Wind answered. "Give me fifteen minutes and I can get the rest finished too."

"You have ten," Rose answered. "Lowell is at The Company training center. Can you link up the detonator to my A.I.?"

"What do you think I am—don't answer that." Wind said, quickly. "You can have remote detonator access pretty much from anywhere in the City. You can also control how much of the charge goes off varying the intensity of the blast. The charges are set sequentially with the parking garage being S1-S3."

"What's the highest section?" Rose asked.

"S7 is the highest and a special surprise for those Company fuckers," Wind answered. "Make sure you aren't in the top levels of the Tower when you detonate S7."

"Pair up the link now, get done, and get the hell out of there," Rose commanded. "Crazy bastard."

"Ten minutes and I'll have her setup," Wind answered. "Remember what I said about Section 7."

Wind then disconnected.

"I thought he said it would take three hours?" I asked as we approached the Tower. "It hasn't been that long has it?"

"He exaggerates to give himself more time to add more explosives," Rose answered. "I'm sure the little shit could've had the entire place wired to blow in an hour or less."

"That is one sick goblin," I noted as we stopped in front of the Tower. We got out of the Hurricane and I looked up. "Do you think they'll let us up?"

"Didn't I tell you?" Rose replied, cracking her neck. "I can be very convincing."

"Ro," Rose said, *"patch in to the explosive array Wind setup and tell me exactly what sections are wired to detonate."*

"Link established," Rowena's voice came over the connector a few seconds later. *"Sections wired to explode are S1 to S3 parking structure adjacent to the Oasis for VIP parking only, S4 to S6 is the Oasis structure itself. Note that S4 to S6 explosions are rigged to create superficial damage while leaving the integrity of the building intact."*

"Smoke and mirrors," Rose said, cutting the connection before Rowena could provide details on S7. "Should be enough to get us Lowell. Are you armed, Chief?"

"Pinky and Butterfly rarely leave my side," I said, patting my lovelies. "I also picked up a blade at Nimble's. One of the Shumants outfitted me with a hellion devastator." I pointed to the blade strapped to my thigh. *"This* is Slice and Dice."

"Why did you choose to give such lame names to your weapons?" Rose asked. "Why not just call them Fluffy Bunny, Pink Unicorn, and my Pointy Stabby?"

"What did you name yours," I asked, feeling slightly offended, "Mayhem and Destruction?"

"My guns," she said, pointing to the handcannons sitting in holsters on either side of her body, "are Lethal

Mercy and Last Word. My blades, Soulsplitter and Divisor."

Those names were much better than mine—shit.

"Rowena," I asked, trying to change the subject of weapons' names, *"shat does Wind have set up with S7?"*

"S7 appears to launch a barrage of missiles—destination: unknown."

"One guess where those missiles are pointed," I said, looking up at the top of the Tower.

"This gets better by the second," Rose remarked, smiling at me. My blood chilled at her expression. "Let's go get us a mage."

CHAPTER 30

We entered the lobby of the Tower and were immediately surrounded by Company security wearing combat armor. They were heavily armed and looked especially twitchy.

The lobby itself was a cavernous space with minimalist design. A large black marble desk, accented with gold flecks matched the marble floor. Behind the desk stood the security captain and beside him were two receptionists.

"Badlands PPD," I said, reaching slowly for my badge. I showed it to the security captain. "I'm Chief Phoenix and I'm here to speak to Leon Ravel."

"Mr. Ravel isn't seeing anyone," the captain answered, barely looking at my badge. "Especially not the PPD. Turn around and go patrol the Strip—while you still can."

See, I knew that the guy had just made Rose's list, but he was still in the dark on that. Something told me that he was super close to finding out what that meant, though.

"Explain to Mr. Ravel," Rose said quietly, "that unless

he wants to be responsible for the destruction of the Oasis, he'll make room in his busy schedule to see us."

"Bullshit," the captain scoffed. "Do you know who the Oasis belongs to?"

"I'm going to guess, Rake Masters?" Rose replied. "Won't *he* be pissed when he finds out you were responsible for destroying his prize property?"

The captain laughed. "What are you going to do? Think nasty thoughts at it?"

Some of the combat armored personnel laughed along with the captain.

That was a mistake.

Not only because they were making Rose even more irritable than she already was, which in and of itself was quite the feat, but also because they were starting to get *my* ire up.

It was one thing to face down a hellion, but it was quite something else to face down a hellion *and* a dragon who were playing on the same team.

"Ro," I heard Rose's voice in my head, *"prepare to detonate the parking structure. Make it messy."*

I covered my ears in preparation of the coming boom boom.

The guards all eyed me in confusion.

"I really hope Mr. Masters doesn't park any expensive vehicles in the Oasis VIP parking garage," Rose said, leaning up against the black marble desk and looking out of the lobby as she, too, brought her hands to her ears. "It would be a shame if the parking structure—I don't know—exploded?"

The captain's face finally registered concern.

"Now, Ro," Rose said. *"Do it."*

The underground VIP parking structure of the Oasis was several blocks away, but the explosion rocked the Strip, sending plumes of water and steam several hundred feet into the air.

The tremors reached us a few seconds later.

"Holy fuck!" yelled the captain, bringing his hands up to his ears far too late. "What the hell did you just do?"

"Who me?" Rose said innocently.

I cracked a smile and stepped up to the captain.

"It's like this, pal," I said, leveling my gaze at him, "you're pissing off the wrong people. We want to see Ravel and we want to see him now."

"Yep," agreed Rose, "I'm pretty sure Mr. Ravel just cleared his schedule to see us. What do *you* think, captain?"

The guy had gone pale as he motioned to the receptionist. "Get Mr. Ravel on the phone." His voice was hoarse. The receptionist was still looking out of the lobby in shock. "Now! Get him on the line now!"

She dialed a number and handed him the phone.

Someone screamed a stream of curses through the earpiece. I put my money on a very disturbed Leon.

"Sir," the captain started, getting in a word between the yells that were coming through the other side of the connection, "the PPD is down here and would like to speak to you."

Rose took the receiver from the shaken captain.

"Hello, Leon," she said sweetly. "Unless you'd like to explain to Mr. Masters how and why his casino just became a pile of rubble on your watch, I'd suggest you clear your schedule."

She handed the receiver back to the captain who remained silent and nodded.

"Mr. Ravel says to stand down and send them up," the captain said. When the combat personnel were slow to comply, he slammed a fist on the black marble desk. "I said stand down!"

The security personnel lowered their weapons and parted for us.

"See? No need for violence," Rose said as we headed for the elevators. "Expert negotiation skills in action."

"Right," I said as I looked out of the lobby at the devastation several blocks away. First responders were already headed to the Oasis. "No violence at all."

CHAPTER 31

*W*e rode up to the forty-seventh floor in silence. The elevator was easily wide enough to fit the Hurricane inside. We both knew the elevators in the Tower would be under surveillance so we did the one thing that would set whoever was watching off.

We checked our weapons.

I ran my hand through my hair and then activated my connector.

"You know they're going to be waiting for us the moment we step off the elevator," I said, making sure both Pinky and Butterfly were loaded with rounds in the chamber.

Rose did the same with her weapons.

"After what happened at the VIP Parking," Rose replied, sorting her speed loaders. *"I doubt they'll try to take us out the moment we enter the office."*

She had a good point.

Leon wouldn't act rashly and eliminate us. He didn't know if we had more explosives set to go off.

"Besides," she continued, *"There's also the problem of killing PPD officers. It's bad for business."*

I scoffed at that. *"Unless that officer happened to be the chief, apparently."*

"It's possible The Company is large enough to eliminate us and suffer little to no repercussions," Rose explained, clearly ignoring my remark, *"but they'd be taking a huge risk."*

Did that mean that not even The Company could survive without the criminal ecosystem that sustained it? My guess was, because of its size, it needed all the other players that indirectly benefitted from The Company's activities.

If they killed us, most of the criminal element of the Badlands would turn their back on them for tainting the water. Granted, as Rose had pointed out, The Company *was* large enough to bury us, both literally and figuratively, but even they couldn't exist on their own.

This didn't mean they wouldn't try, though.

We just needed to make them understand that giving us Lowell was the lesser of two evils. The third option was the least desirable. They could opt to kill us and erase Lowell as a liability.

We were relying on the fact that Leon enjoyed eating solid food and having a pulse.

If the PPD destroyed the Oasis, more than the destruction of a prized property, which it was, it would make The Company look weak. It was the unspoken corollary to the first law of the Badlands.

Hilda's words came back to me: *"The first law in the Badlands is kill or be killed. You're a dragon being raised by valkyrie, so you must understand the second law if you are to survive this land."*

"How many laws are there?" I'd mistakenly asked at the time.

A swift punch to the stomach followed by a hard slap across the face knocked me off my feet and sent me sliding across the training area.

"Two," she continued. *"The second law is: only the strong and the clever survive. If you can't be one, make sure you are the other. If you want to be truly feared and respected—be both."*

Rake Masters was both.

He was the lynchpin to our entire strategy.

They needed to fear Rake enough not to anger him. Losing the Oasis would piss him off spectacularly. More importantly, the perceived weakness of losing the flagship property would be like releasing a mob of blood imps on the Strip. The Company would be the victim of a bloodbath as every competitor waiting in the shadows made their move.

Sometimes being the largest only served to make you a huge target.

The first victim after the Oasis fell would be Leon, followed swiftly by every member of the PPD.

Rake would need to make a statement—a loud, violent, and bloody one.

We didn't need a war.

I didn't want a war.

But an entity as large and ruthless as The Company wasn't going to listen to us unless we got their attention. The only way to do that was to threaten a war of total annihilation.

Fortunately, for me, I had an expert negotiator on my team.

Rose was well versed in the languages of death, destruction, and mayhem. I just had to tactfully unleash her on Leon and make sure she didn't drink whatever it was Pytha had given her.

"You do the talking," I said under my breath, but loud enough for Rose to hear. "I got your six until I need to take point. Then we unleash hell."

Rose drew her guns, I popped my scales and pulled Butterfly as the elevator doors opened, and the world exploded.

CHAPTER 32

The small rocket punched me in the chest, flinging me to the rear of the elevator car, before it exploded in my face. Rose dove out and rolled to the side, firing her guns at the combat personnel around us.

Smoke billowed out of the elevator and obscured my vision.

I staggered out and fell forward narrowly missing catching another rocket in the face.

It was clear Leon wasn't worried about the consequences of killing PPD officers.

"Fuck you, Rose!" screamed a voice from the other side of the room. "We caught your little shit of a goblin. Did you think it was going to be that easy?"

I crawled along the floor to where Rose sat behind an overturned sofa.

"Not bad, Chief," Rose said with a nod as she readied her handcannons. "Now we know you can withstand small rockets. Good job. We'll try larger ones once we get back to Nimble's."

"Can we focus on the asshole trying to kill us first?" I asked with a gasp.

"Good point," Rose said, firing back at the security personnel. "We just want to talk, Leon!"

"I've heard about your *conversations*, Rose," Leon yelled back. "I'll pass, thanks."

"Seems like your negotiation skills precede you, Lieutenant," I said, getting the feeling back in my chest. "Probably because all your negotiations end with casualties?"

"Let's not nitpick over insignificant details, Chief," Rose objected. "I get results. And that's all that matters."

My chest throbbed in pain. The explosion was minor, but the impact was enough of a kick to force the air out of my lungs. I sat still for a second trying to catch my breath.

Bullets tore into the wall and floor around us. In a few seconds the sofa we were using as cover would be shredded fabric and offer about as much protection as a piece of toilet paper.

"I *felt* that rocket," I said with a groan, drawing Pinky. "Do we need this Leon alive? Because I'm seriously considering retiring him permanently after that rocket reception."

A smile slowly crossed Rose's face.

"Mostly dead and slightly alive works too," she said. "Leon is the only one who has the access codes to the training area and Lowell. We need him alive long enough to get them."

Another rocket shot by us and exploded in the elevator.

The smoke in the room made visibility near zero, but I didn't need to rely on my sight. I was a dragon and it was time I acted like one.

I expanded my senses and silenced everything around me. Using my hearing, I focused on the source of the rocket launcher. I heard another rocket being pushed into the tube.

Firing multiple dragon rounds wasn't possible, *unless* you disabled the safety. It required multiple thumb-clicks to get it done, but under the circumstances, I worked through them.

I rolled to the side and fired Pinky once, twice, and a third time in a spread pattern—the one thing I was never supposed to do. The barrel of the shotgun became white hot. I tossed it across the room as I grabbed Rose and threw her in the elevator car.

"What the fu—?" I heard her say as she landed hard and the other side of the room erupted in flame. "Unholy hell, what did you just do?"

"Fired Pinky one time too many," I said, running into the elevator behind her. "Three explosive rounds in succession and the residue in the barrel sets off a chain reaction. The whole weapon explodes."

"You intentionally carry a weapon that can *explode* on you if fired more than once at a time?"

"Makes life interesting," I said. "Keeps me on my toes."

"Wait, I thought you couldn't fire that one multiple times?"

"You can't," I replied, "unless you go through the hassle of taking of the multi-fire safety."

"Which you clearly did."

"Had to be done."

"And here I was think you to be one of the least suicidal on the team," Rose rasped, moving out of the line of fire.

I pressed Whoosh, formed my wings, and crouched down in the car next to her as a barrage of rockets came our way.

"I really hope my wings are strong enough to deal with this," I said, clenching my teeth against the impending impact.

Several of the rockets missed, but enough of them hit their mark.

The projectiles slammed into the elevator. I wrapped my wings around us as the impact and explosions buffeted the car.

After a few seconds, the rockets stopped. The smoke cleared and I saw Leon behind a plexan shield.

Most of his combat personnel were scattered around the office, either dead or wounded. Groans filled the room from the survivors as Leon put down the phone and glared at us.

Leon was average-sized. Dressed in a black business suit with a weak chin and a strong receding hairline. His beady eyes radiated malice and intelligence. I could tell he was the type who rose through The Company ranks by betraying or eliminating whomever he needed to in his quest for power.

"Nice try, Rose," Leon said, with a sneer. "It was great

meeting you, Chief Phoenix. Sorry to drop you like this, but I have non-explosive meetings to attend. I'll make sure to send Windham, your explosive little shit of a friend, back to the PPD—in pieces. The fucker cost me a fortune in vehicles."

"I'm going to end you, Leon," Rose said, pushing my wings out of the way and firing several rounds into the plexan with no effect. "You and Lowell will die today."

"Sorry to disappoint," Leon answered, shaking his head. "We're The Company, remember? We didn't get to where we are by being easy targets. We prepare for every contingency."

He reached under his desk.

The elevator door slammed shut boxing us in with a bang.

"What the—?" I said moving back and looking around us. "The walls."

"What about them?" Rose snapped. "Are you an interior decorator now?"

"What your observant Chief is trying to tell you is that there is no exit from the elevator," Leon said over the intercom. "Also, I'm not exactly versed in physics, but I don't think a hellion *or* a dragon can withstand a drop from forty-seven stories."

"A drop?" Rose said, looking around. "Leon, you're starting to piss me off."

"Killing a PPD officer will open you up to prosecution to the fullest extent of the law," I said, hoping that was true. "You don't want to do this. Just give us Mage Lowell and we can resolve this situation amicably."

Laughter erupted over the intercom.

"Are you for real?" Leon said in-between gasps. "*You're* going to prosecute The Company? We *are* the law, making us assuredly above it."

"No one is above the law," I said, letting the anger flow through me. "No one."

"*Get ready, Rose,*" I said over the communicator. "*He's going to cut us loose.*"

"*Fuck? You mean—?*"

I heard a muffled explosion above us and then the loud snap. Leon had just cut the cables holding the elevator.

He had just dropped us.

CHAPTER 33

My valkyrie mother had devised training exercises to help me form my wings and learn flight under pressure and stress. It consisted of taking me to progressively higher points around our land and pushing me off the edge.

Valkyrie training—you have to love it.

She had a name for this exercise that I grew to loathe. She called it 'Drop the Dragon' and all the valkyrie enjoyed it. I must have broken every limb at least once, until I learned how to scale my body. Then it was just a matter of severe bruising. After some time, I grew strong enough that I didn't even bruise.

The last day of the 'Drop the Dragon' Hilda took me to Heaven's Fang. One of the highest mountains in the Netherworld. She drew her sword and walked me to the edge.

"Today you fly or die," she said and lunged at me, forcing me off the edge.

For a few seconds, I considered not even trying to form my wings as the ground raced up at me.

That's when I felt the rage.

The anger I had kept pushed down and controlled—broke free. It was subtle at first. A simple surge of power until I let it go and it consumed me. I channeled it and redirected it into my body.

It was as though a memory had been unlocked and the fullness of my ability to fly had returned.

My wings formed and I flew back to the top of Heaven's Fang.

I proudly showed my wings to Hilda, who nodded approvingly, waited until I calmed down, and retracted my wings. She then proceeded to kick me off the edge again.

"Once is an accident," she yelled as I fell to my death again. "Twice is a habit. Fly or die, boy!"

Valkyrie parenting—not for the weak.

From that day, there had been flashes of the past, glimpses of a life where I had flown with others of my kind. Dreams followed, but they were weak and I could never remember them. I assumed that one day it would all come rushing back to me, but that day was not today.

Grabbing the railing on the wall, I pulled myself down and removed several Pinky shells from my pockets. I tossed them towards the ceiling, causing them to stick in place.

"What are you doing?" Rose's voice came over in my head.

Even in a falling elevator and plunging to our apparent demise, she still managed to sound irritated.

Hellions were insane.

"Get behind me," I said as I drew Butterfly aiming at the shells. *"We need an exit."*

"You waiting for a countdown?" Rose asked. *"Shoot them!"*

She scrambled behind me as the shells detonated and blew a hole in the roof of the elevator. I grabbed her and pushed up letting my wings keep us aloft. The elevator car continued down the shaft.

I looked up at the opening on the forty-seventh floor.

"Let's go get us a mage," I said and lifted us up the shaft.

We heard the crash of the elevator a few seconds later as the car impacted the ground floor and created an enormous cloud of dust and debris below us.

"Make sure they're dead!" Leon's voice carried over to us in the shaft. "I want to see the bloody pieces of that hellion bitch, Rose."

"Seems like he really likes you," I said, approaching the open elevator doors above us. *"Why not return the sentiment?"*

"Exactly what I was thinking," Rose said with a wicked grin. *"If we can hear him this clearly, his plexan blast shield is down. Can you launch me in there?"*

"Launch you?"

"Yes, throw me in—fast," Rose said, making sure her guns were loaded. *"It's the last thing he'll expect."*

"He isn't the only one," I said, turning in a circle and releasing her as I ascended the shaft. *"Don't kill him—yet."*

I flew in after my partner as she sailed across the office and landed on Leon's chest, both guns pointing at his face.

"Hello, you slimy fucker," Rose barked. "Bet you didn't prepare for *this* contingency."

CHAPTER 34

"*I* should put two in you and call it a day," Rose snarled. "You let that fuck Lowell try to dust us—not once, but twice."

"Don't kill him—yet." I said, retracting my wings.

Leon looked completely terrified as Rose remained perched on his chest. I knew it could be an act. He didn't get to be in his position without being clever and dangerous.

Hilda used to always say: *"Even a cornered mouse will attack, unless you crush it with your boot until its head explodes."*

"Rowena," I said through my connector, *"wide channel, please."*

"Officer Chat enabled, Chief," Rowena answered. *"Would you like me to coordinate with the first responders at the Oasis?"*

"No, let Butch and Silk handle the mess over at the Oasis," I replied. *"Coordinate with Lieutenant Fand and see if Wind is still on the premises. Graffon, you and Doe join up with us at the Tower, wait for the medical team, and contact The Morgue. We have dead and injured up here."*

"Got it, Chief," Graffon responded. *"Is Leon still alive?"*

"For now," I answered. *"Rose is going to have some words with him about getting to Lowell."*

"Oh shit," Silk said. *"Better tell The Morgue it's plus one."*

I looked around at the destruction that had transformed Leon's office. Bullet holes, spent rounds, craters in walls, and bodies were everywhere.

I was standing in the middle of a war zone.

In the corner, I saw what was left of Pinky, picked it up, and holstered the remains of my shotgun. I'd have Nimble take a look at it and see if it could be restored.

Rose and Leon hadn't moved an inch. Well, Rose hadn't, but her guns had. One was aimed at Leon's crotch and the other rested on his forehead. Both hammers were cocked back. Leon was ten pounds of pressure away from losing his head—both of them.

"You tried to drop us down an elevator shaft," I said calmly, sitting on the edge of his desk. "That wasn't cool, Leon. Not cool at all." I then tapped on the barrel of the gun that was sticking to his head. "We need access to Mage Lowell, Leon. Think you might want to help us now?"

"You don't know what you're asking," Leon pleaded, his eyes strained. "I can't give you that information. Masters would kill me."

"Master's isn't currently in the position to make you a lobotomized eunuch like someone else I know," I educated him, leaning my head toward Rose. "You know what I'm saying?"

"Uh…"

"I'll spell it out for you," I said in a helpful tone of voice. "You see, Masters *may* kill you, whereas Rose *will* kill you. Between you and me," I added, bringing my head closer toward his, "I think she's probably most interested in blowing your dick off."

"Phrasing," muttered Rose.

Leon's eyes widened even more.

I sat back up and clasped my hands together.

"Now, I'm sure the PPD could offer some kind of—?"

"Of what?" Leon asked, letting out a dry laugh. "Protection? From Rake Masters and The Company? Are you really that clueless?"

I looked up at Rose who shook her head.

"This fucker is dead," she said, her voice grim. "Not a matter of *if*, but *when* Masters dusts his ass. At this point it'd probably be a piece of mercy for me to just kill him now."

"What?" Leon blurted.

"In that case," I said, walking away to face the windows that overlooked the Strip, "we may as well do them both a favor."

"What?" Leon said again.

"I mean, if Leon doesn't have any information we can use, what good is he?"

"True," Rose replied.

"Wait a minute, what are you talking about?" Leon asked, his voice laced with fear. "You don't understand, you can't protect me. No one can! And why are you talking about me as if I'm not even here?"

"Erase his ass, Rose."

"Are you serious?" Rose asked over the communicator. *"This is a little dark even for a dragon. I mean, don't get me wrong, I'd* love *to delete this fucker, but I thought you were the by-the-book type. I don't want to be accused of—"*

"Rose," I interrupted, *"of course I don't want you to actually kill him. He's just so focused on Masters that he's not getting the real threat he's faced with here. He sees us as cops and so he doesn't think we'll actually go through with wiping his ass out. But he doesn't know me, which means he has no idea if I'm bluffing or not."*

"Gotcha," Rose said. *"I gotta say, Chief, that I'm pretty impressed with you right now."*

"Then my life is complete," I snarked.

"Nice. Okay, roll with me on this." Then, she said aloud, "Are you sure, Chief? I mean, you know damn well that *I'm* a huge fan of killing him right now, but I'm not cleaning up the mess."

"I don't care," I said, my voice hard as I spun and walked back to them. "No code means he's worthless." I was now pointing at him as if he were nothing but a tool. "This was a waste of time. We have better things to do than sit around with this slice of lunchmeat."

"What?" they both said in unison, giving me a baffled look.

Okay, so maybe that wasn't the best insult.

"Do it," I commanded.

Rose shrugged and looked back down at Leon.

A few seconds later, she jumped away from him, looking disgusted.

"Dude," she yelled, "did I feel what I think I just felt?"

Leon's hands went down to cover his groin.

"What's going on?" I asked.

"Leon just got wood."

My look of disgust joined Rose's.

"You got a boner, dude?"

"It's called a 'stress erection'," he replied, his face turning beet red. "It's not nice to make fun."

Rose and I dropped our grimaces, replacing them with grins. Soon after, laughter ensued. It was all we could do to keep our composure.

"This is perfect," I said, my stomach aching from laughter. "We don't have to kill him, after all."

Rose snorted.

Yes, actually snorted.

"What are you talking about?" Leon raged, his hands still covering his crotch.

It took me a few seconds to calm down enough to tell him, but even then, I was finding it a challenge to talk.

"We've got something on you that's worse than death, Leon," I said, wiping my eyes. "If you don't help us, we'll tell everyone that you've got a serious case of... gun...boner!"

Rose hit the floor, curling up in a ball as laughter racked her body.

"You wouldn't dare!" hissed Leon.

That only made us laugh harder. Honestly, I hadn't had this much fun...ever.

"That would ruin me," Leon pleaded. "My reputation...my legacy!"

"It'd definitely change your legacy, Lord Nervy Priapism!" Rose roared.

"Bahahahaha," I replied, putting my hands on my knees, nearly heaving.

I was dying here, but I had to get my wits about me, and so did Rose. Leon was clearly not in a position to do anything against us right now.

His hands were occupied.

But if he suddenly caught on that Rose and I were equally incapacitated due to laughter, he may figure out a means to get away or exact some sort of revenge.

As if on cue, he jumped off the table.

I leveled Butterfly at him.

"No, no," I rasped. "I'm still quite capable of filling you with holes."

"Don't tell him that," Rose howled, "he might bust a nut!"

"Bahahahaha," I bellowed in response, but kept Butterfly focused at him.

"You two are a couple of assholes," Leon scolded us. "I can't believe it. You're like children."

"Says the guy who gets spontaneous erections," I quipped.

"Bahahahaha," Rose belted out.

Leon's face was a mix of rage and worry.

To be fair, I couldn't blame him. If I got 'stress erections', I'd probably do everything I could to keep it a secret, too.

"*Okay, okay,*" I said to Rose. "*We have to get back to work now.*"

"*This is fucking priceless. I haven't laughed like this in years.*"

"*I know,*" I replied. "*Me too, but let's get serious.*"

"*I'll try.*"

"*Yeah.*"

Rose got to her feet and wiped the tears from her face.

It was good to see her with a look that wasn't predicated on killing someone.

"You *can't* tell anyone," Leon whimpered. "It will destroy how people have viewed me."

"Well, now," I said, my breathing still a bit ragged, "that will all depend on how helpful you are."

"What about Hilda?" Rose asked, still doing her best to fight down the giggle loop we were both engaged in. "Wouldn't she take him in?" She then looked down at his pants. "I didn't mean it like that."

"Hilda?" I asked, looking over at Leon, my glee instantly fading at the thought. "Why would she help Company scum?"

"They have no love for Masters or The Company," Rose replied. "I'm sure with a word from you they could take him in and hide him. Masters would never move against the valkyries—no one is that crazy, not even him."

A spark of hope gleamed in Leon's eyes.

"You know valkyries?" he asked. "Real ones?"

Rose chuckled again, but held herself in check.

"My mother is a valkyrie," I answered. "You give us the code for the training center and I can take you to them within the hour."

Leon grabbed a sheet of paper and scribbled something down fast. He handed the paper to Rose.

"That's it," Leon said. "Let's go to the valkyries—now."

"Once I get confirmation of the code," I remarked. "If it clears, we'll relocate to the valkyries."

"It'll clear."

"We'll see." I then turned to Rose, but avoided looking into her eyes because I knew that would only cause us both to burst into laughter again. "Send that code to Nimble and get positive confirmation."

She nodded.

"Chief," Rowena said in my head, *"I'm registering activity on S7. I suggest exiting the premises immediately. I no longer have control over the explosives array."*

Rose clearly heard the warning, too, as she looked up at me concerned.

"Leon, is there another way out of this office?" she asked. "Is the elevator the only—?"

"The elevator is the only way in and out of this office," Leon said. "It's how I controlled access. Mr. Masters insisted on it."

"Shit," Rose said, looking at the destroyed elevator shaft, her laughter eradicated by Rowena's warning. "We have a problem."

"What's wrong?" Leon asked, looking around and getting agitated. "It's Masters isn't it? He knows. Somehow, he knows I'm here talking to you."

"Calm down, Leon," I said. "Your pants are already tight enough." I then tilted my head at him. "Wait, how would Masters know?"

"You don't know Masters," Leon answered, rubbing his hand through his thinning hair. "He knows. I'm dead. I'm so dead."

"Chief, the missile array has been recalibrated," Rowena said in my ear. *"Verifying new coordinates now."*

"No need Rowena," I said. *"I'm pretty sure I know where*

they are headed."

"Coordinates verified," Rowena replied. *"The missiles are currently pointed at your location and will impact thirty seconds from launch."*

"Can you carry us both down the elevator shaft?" Rose asked, looking at Leon. *"He's scum that deserves to die, but not like this. Plus, I'd like to stop Masters for once."*

"I've never had to carry more than one person," I said.

"He's got a handle," Rose said, her face threatening to break again into laughter.

That's how you know you have the right person on your squad. If they're laughing in the face of death, they've got their priorities straight.

"We need to go," I said, "before Masters finds out you've spoken to us."

Leon nodded. "Yes, yes that's a good idea," he agreed. "But how? The elevator is destroyed."

I formed my wings behind me.

Leon backed away fear in his eyes. "You're going to carry the both of us?" he asked raising his voice. "Down forty-seven stories?"

"Yes," I said. "I can do this. You don't want to stay here, trust me."

Leon shook his head and backed away even more.

"I don't trust you, no," Leon shot back. "You want me dead. You'll let me go and call it an accident."

"Missiles have been launched, Chief," Rowena said in my head. *"Would you like a countdown to impact?"*

"No thank you, Rowena," I answered. *"Just let me know at the ten second mark."*

"We need to get the fuck out of here now," Rose rasped. *"He*

can take his chances behind his plexan. I don't feel like being blown to bits. Let's go."

"Leon," I said, keeping my voice even and outstretching an arm, "you'll have a better chance with us."

"Fuck you, dragon," he spat. "I'll take my chances here."

Leon pressed a section of his desk and the plexan shield shot up.

"That won't be enough," I said, backing up to the elevator shaft. "Last chance."

"I hope Lowell burns you to ash," Leon replied with a sneer.

"Whatever you say, boner boy," I scoffed. "You might want to hurry up and knock one out, though. The end is coming."

"Phrasing," Rose chuckled.

"Fuck you, asshole," Leon roared. "Fuck both of you!"

"He probably could, too," I noted to Rose.

She started to lose it again.

"Don't worry, Leon," I called out as I grabbed Rose and stepped into the open space of the elevator shaft, "we'll be sure your tombstone reads, 'The guy was a real stiff'!"

CHAPTER 35

*W*e were falling fast.

No amount of 'Drop the Dragon' prepared me for falling down an elevator shaft carrying a hellion while we avoided being incinerated by a swarm of missiles.

Badlands PPD—where the excitement is literally red-hot.

"Impact in ten seconds," Rowena said in my head. *"Please seek cover."*

"We're heading down an elevator shaft on the North side of the Tower," I said, making sure I didn't drop Rose. *"There's no cover to seek."*

"Taking an elevator with an impending missile strike is inadvisable," Rowena answered. *"Please egress using the stairs."*

I kept my wings close to my body and allowed gravity to pull us down. About halfway, I opened them slightly and increased the surface area to slow our fall. The strain was immense. It felt like a troll was trying to remove my wings one at a time.

An explosion rocked the top of the Tower and I saw a fireball make its way down the shaft after us. I pulled my wings tight again and accelerated our drop. We left the fireball behind but the destroyed elevator was waiting for us below.

I opened my wings and gritted my teeth against the pain. We slowed and landed with a crash onto the elevator car, denting the roof and missing the opening I had created by inches. I rolled over and into the elevator with a groan. We fell into the car with a thud as my wings retracted.

"Holy shit!" a paramedic, one of the first responders, jumped back in surprise. "Where did you come from?"

A group of first responders stood around the destroyed elevator.

"PPD," Rose said, flashing her badge. "Get your men out of here it's not safe."

"I was just about to say the same thing to you, ma'am," the paramedic replied, grabbing me by the shoulder and pulling. "This elevator is unstable, it could—"

Rose looked up, grabbed the paramedic by the shirt, and flung him down the corridor. She turned, grabbed me by the arm, and pulled me out of the elevator as a mass of debris crashed onto the car, crushing it further.

"Don't ma'am me," Rose scolded the shaken paramedic, "and get your men to set up a perimeter. The top of this building was just blasted by a missile strike."

"Missile strike?" the paramedic asked in shock. "We

were just told the elevator malfunctioned and dropped. No one said anything about a missile strike!"

"*I'm* telling you now," Rose snapped. "Get your team. Set up a perimeter and contact Lieutenant Fand over at Fire Control. Tell him Lieutenant Blaze from the PPD is requesting Fire Team at the top of the Tower."

"Yes, ma'am," the paramedic replied before running off.

Rose propped me up as we left the lobby. I'd forgotten how strong hellions were as she helped me out of the building with little effort.

"Let's not do that again," I groaned.

"You could have stayed in the office a little longer, Chief," Rose replied with a wicked smile. "We could have tested you against those missiles."

"Eat shit and die, Lieutenant," I shot back. "No offense."

"It's good to see I've been such a positive influence on you," Rose laughed, looking up as we stepped outside of the Tower. "I don't think Leon made it."

I followed her gaze up and realized she was right. The top two floors of the Tower weren't on fire—they were gone.

"No," I agreed, "but I wonder if his erection did."

She dropped me.

CHAPTER 36

"*W*ell, shit," I said, gingerly sliding into the Hurricane to avoid aggravating the bruise that was my body. "Leon should've accepted my offer."

"He was dead," Rose said, starting the engine, her giggles slowly fading away. "It was just a matter of time. I will, however, give Masters kudos. Death by missile is a creative method of elimination."

"You seriously think he was behind this?" I asked.

"Certainly follows his M.O. of not leaving evidence behind," Rose said, tapping into her connector. *"Nimble, confirmation on the code I sent you?"*

"Looks legitimate," Nimble's voice came in over the channel. *"The code appears to give access to a secret Company training facility called the Killbox. Doesn't sound inviting. Maybe postpone the visit?"*

"Lowell is hiding there," Rose answered. *"I need to go over and make him dead."*

"You know where this Killbox place is?" I asked,

tightening my grip on the door handle as she swerved around traffic. "And are we trying to die *before* we get there?"

"*Chief,*" Nimble said in my head, "*you have an urgent call at the office.*"

"*Can Rowena patch it into my connector?*" I asked, confused as to why Nimble would inform me of a call. "*Makes no sense to go back to HQ when we're already on the road.*"

"*This is a Director call,*" Nimble replied. I saw Rose grimace as she made a U-turn on the busy Strip, nearly causing several accidents. "*No patching in. It's a live call in your office. Chief only.*"

Nimble hung up and Rose cursed again.

"That seems inefficient," I remarked as Rose increased the speed. "Why not just patch it through?"

"Safety mostly," Rose answered. "They have their meetings over a VPN—virtual private network, with enough encryption to make Rowena look like two cans and a string."

"Sounds impressive," I said. "Have you ever spoken to the Directors?"

"Have I ever been chief?" Rose glanced at me. "Did you smash your skull when your head dented the elevator?"

"This isn't exactly the best time to have a meeting," I started. "I mean—"

"They call, you go," Rose answered, flexing the muscles in her jaw and gripping the steering wheel hard enough to leave a slight imprint. "Part of the job. Especially for PPD chiefs."

Fine. So there was no way around this. It had to happen sooner or later, I just would have preferred later. Though, honestly, it probably should have been sooner.

"While I'm having this meeting, round up the team," I commanded. "Make sure they're outfitted and prepped to head to the Killbox."

We arrived at PPD HQ and I entered my new office. It wasn't overly large. A tall filing cabinet sat to one side of the room. A good-sized desk sat in the center of the room. The desk held a computer, some stacks of paper I wasn't looking forward to reviewing, and a phone.

I looked around expecting some sign as to where this meeting was supposed to take place.

"Nimble," I said using my connector, *"where is this Director's meeting supposed to be?"*

"I got this one, slug," Silk's voice chimed in. *"Hey, Chief. Step out of your office and head downstairs."*

"I thought it was supposed to be in my office?"

"They changed it because of security," Silk answered. *"Take one flight down, make a right, at the end of the corridor take another right. First door on the left. The door won't have any markings since only the officers know about these kinds of meetings."*

I followed the instructions and found myself in front of a bare metal door.

"I'm here, now what?"

"Just walk in," Silk answered. *"They'll be waiting for you."*

I opened the door and was greeted with a group of screams and curses. Followed by the burst of laughter over the connector.

"Get the hell out of here you pervert!" screamed one of the women who was standing in front of me in a state of undress. "Don't you know how to read?"

Silk had led me to a PPD female locker room.

CHAPTER 37

"*T*hat was hilarious, team," I said, once I got back to my office. "*Thank you for that singular experience. I'll remember how special it felt when I start giving out patrol assignments. I hear the fae enjoy walking the sewers of Infernal City. Plenty of crime down there to deter.*"

"*Did he say sewers?*" Butch asked, quickly. "*Chief, I'd like to put in a formal request for a new partner.*"

"*No need,*" I said, calmly. "*Since no one felt the need to warn me, I think everyone will have the pleasure of spending some time down there. I hear walking through a river of waste is perfect for team character building.*"

"*Fucking Silk,*" I heard Rose's voice. "*If I have to patrol the sewers because of you, I'm ripping off the important bits from your scrawny ass.*"

A chorus of 'fucking Silk' came across the connector.

The shared agony made me smile.

"*I have a meeting with the Directors in my office,*" I said. "*Get it together. Once I'm done, we retire Lowell with extreme prejudice.*"

A chorus of, *"Yes, Sir,"* was the response.

I hung up the group channel.

"Rowena, where am I supposed to have this Director's meeting?"

"There is an adjacent space to the rear of your office, Chief," Rowena said in my ear. *"That space is to be utilized for all Director meetings."*

"Thank you," I said, irritated. *"I could have used that information ten minutes ago."*

"You didn't ask me directly."

"Right," I said. *"In the future feel free to share pertinent information with me without my having to ask your directly for it."*

"Please use the panel on the wall for access," Rowena said. *"It is keyed to your biometrics."*

I placed my hand on the wall and a panel slid to the side revealing a small room with a desk, a large comfortable chair and three monitors attached to the far wall. There was nothing else in the room.

I sat in the chair and the monitors turned on.

Silhouetted and obscured figures appeared in each of the monitors.

"Good afternoon, Ezekias," said the figure on the right. "We understand you just came from the Tower?"

"I was just *exploded* out of the Tower," I replied. "I don't know if I'd use the term 'good' to describe this day."

"Really, Long," the figure on the left said, "was that supposed to be a joke?"

"Not at all," Long answered. "I was just trying to ascertain how he felt."

"Baked," I muttered. "Having rockets fired at me is not my idea of fun."

"We'll get straight to the point then, Chief Phoenix," the center figure said. "We called you here to discuss some matters that have come to our attention. I am Taragon, to your left is Ellium, and on your right is Long. Together we represent the three major factions of the Badlands."

Above each monitor was a name placard. It matched what Taragon had said. That was good seeing as how there was no way I'd remember their faces, especially since I couldn't really see them.

"What matters?" I asked politely, realizing these were my bosses.

"You contracted a certain goblin," Ellium started, "Windham, to detonate property belonging to one Rake Masters?"

"Detonate is a strong word," I countered. "We needed information from Leon, one of Masters' men."

"And you felt it was appropriate to destroy private property to obtain this information?" Long asked.

"When my team and I are being targeted for assassination, yes, I did," I answered. "Leon had the means to get us into the location where we believe a suspect is hiding."

"Targeted for assassination?" Taragon asked. "Isn't it true that *you* were the only one being targeted?"

Was this a meeting or an interrogation? I was sitting there dealing with three people who were hiding behind screens, all while a rogue mage was out there killing people.

I didn't have time for this nonsense.

"Yes, sir," I answered. "Most of the attacks were directed at me. At first it was thought it was part of a funeral party, which is apparently a lethal hazing every chief seemingly goes through. I don't recall seeing that in the employee manual, though."

"We are familiar with the practice," Taragon replied, "and we're all quite impressed that you've survived as long as you have. Now, what made you think it was more than a funeral party?"

Nice.

It was bad enough that my crew kicked my ass with practical jokes, ribbing me about their assumption that I wouldn't be around long, and giving me next to no information about how to do my job, but now I had three bosses who held just as little faith in my ability to survive as my crew.

There was no time for me to hold a personal pity party, though.

"The first victim was a hellion diplomat," I explained, "followed by assassination attempts in different locations and culminating with the death of Emissary Sinclair."

"You're sure all these deaths were connected?" Long asked. "It could be you're just trying to find a connection that didn't exist."

"All were the work of one Mage Lowell," I answered, trying to maintain my composure. "He is currently in the employ of The Company. I was about to apprehend the subject when you summoned me to this meeting."

"Apprehend?" Taragon asked. "As in arrest and incarcerate? Or the method your hellion lieutenant is known for—shoot first and don't bother with the questions?"

"Lieutenant Blaze is an exemplary officer of the PPD," I replied, irked they would try to insult Rose.

I mean, it *was* true she was psychotic and most likely mildly sociopathic, but she was *my* second-in-command. I wasn't going to have some armchair Director, who probably never spent a day in the field, call her character into question.

Whatever she was, she was PPD first.

"Do you know why we're having this meeting?" Taragon asked.

Besides wasting my time?

"No, sir," I replied, "but I'm sure you're going to inform me."

"Indeed," Taragon answered. "You have zero experience as an officer of the PPD, but you were the only dragon available who was insane enough to take the position, and dragons were slated as next-in-line for leading the PPD. That means we want to be informed every step of the way."

"Understood, sir," I said. "I will strive to do my best to honor the faith you've placed in me."

"Your first week and you're going after Masters?" Ellium asked. "I believe you're biting off more than you can chew."

"Are you implying Rake Masters is above the law?" I let a small amount of the anger seep into my voice. "Is that what this is about? I'm stepping on Company toes?"

"We're merely warning you to pick your battles wisely, Chief Phoenix," Taragon answered. "You may find that the tail of the cat you're grabbing actually belongs to a tiger. Tread carefully."

"No one is above the law—no one." I said, my voice steel. "If that's all, I have a rogue mage suspect to *apprehend*."

"That will be all for now, Chief," Taragon answered. "Be safe out there."

The monitors went dark and the door behind me slid open.

CHAPTER 38

"*R*owena," I said, leaving my office, *"group channel."*

I headed downstairs to the tech station.

"How'd they treat you, Chief?" Silk was the first to speak. *"Did you get any special Director knowledge?"*

"Can you share it with us?" Butch chimed in. *"Help us all be wise, Chief. You're our only hope."*

The team erupted in laughter. I knew what it was and let them have their moment. We were about to face a skilled high-level Mage who worked for The Company, managed to escape capture, and tried to kill us several times.

Gallows humor was just one way to deal with life threatening situations. Going to a secret training facility named the Killbox only drove the point home.

This was life or death.

"Hilarious," I answered with a chuckle of my own. *"Rose and I will take point on this Killbox location. I'm going to make a stop at Nimble's and meet up with the Lieutenant in ten."*

"Roger that," Rose said. *"Let's go, bitches."*

"I love it when she sweet-talks us," Silk answered.

"Designations are as follows," Rose said in a clipped voice. *"Me and the chief are PPD 1. Graffon and Doe, PPD 2. Butch and Silk, PPD 3. Get in your vehicles. We leave as soon as the chief meets up with me."*

The panel to the Tech Station had been replaced with a setup similar to the one I had in my office. I placed my hand on it and winced. The last time I did that, a demolition team had to be called in. This time the door whispered open, letting me in.

Yarrl and Tam were busy at separate workstations and ignored my entrance. I was certain they had determined who was at the door long before it opened and gave me access.

I unholstered my damaged shotgun and stepped over to Nimble.

"Can you do anything with this?" I asked showing him the mangled remains of Pinky.

"You mean besides melting it down?" Nimble extended an eyestalk and examined Pinky closely. "That weapon is scrap."

"Can you restore it?" I asked. "It has sentimental value."

"Tam?" Nimble called out and Tam was behind me before I could sense her presence. "She's the one who can tell you if it is salvageable."

Sneaking up on a dragon required incredible skill. A dragon's heightened senses operated several levels beyond most species. Only hellions matched us, and even then, it was nearly impossible to sneak up on a dragon. If we didn't hear you, we smelled you coming.

Tam had just managed to impress and creep me out all at the same time. It also made me realize this pair of hellions could pose a real threat.

I made a mental note to research House Manusht.

Tam stood in front of me and held out her hand. I placed Pinky in it and she proceeded to examine what was left of my shotgun. She turned the weapon over several times before nodding.

"Do you have any of the dragon rounds for this weapon?" Tam asked, looking at me. "One or two should suffice."

I reached in the pocket of my coat and pulled out several of the rounds I hadn't used at the Tower.

"Here you go," I said, placing them in her hand. "Why do you need them?"

"Two weeks," Tam said.

"Two weeks?" I asked. "Are you serious?"

"I will have a modified and upgraded version for you by then," Tam replied, before walking away to the workstation she'd stood at earlier.

"Thank you," I said. "I thought it was gone."

She nodded and then proceeded to ignore me.

"You're headed to the Killbox," Nimble noted, typing on the keyboard.

I nodded. "That's where Lowell is hiding. We need to bring him in."

"You may want to see this, then," Nimble said, pointing to the screen. "The entire facility sits on top of a barracks."

"Shit," I said. "How many?"

"If they're running exercises," Nimble mused, "they'll

have several full security details on the premises. About thirty to forty combat security personnel, I would guess."

"I'm going to need a backup weapon to replace Pinky," I grunted, looking at the schematics of the Killbox. "Do you have another shotgun?"

"Pinky?" Nimble asked incredulous. "You named your weapon...Pinky? What happened, Cottonball was taken?"

Everyone was a comedian.

"Do you have something or not?" I asked, losing my patience.

"Tam can outfit you with a replacement weapon," Nimble answered, "though I don't think it will be nearly as fearsome as a shotgun named Pinky."

"Hilarious," I replied. "Another shotgun will do just fine."

"Are you sure you want to do this?" Nimble asked as Tam handed me another weapon. "Wouldn't it be better to lure this mage out instead of walking into the Killbox?"

"Thirty to forty combat security against six PPD?" I asked as a smile crossed my lips, scanning over the new shotgun. Clearly, I had spent too much time around Rose. "Those sound like great odds."

CHAPTER 39

*W*e drove into the desolation at the edge of hellion territory.

The Killbox was located outside Infernal City, and it had a nice view of the distant Dragon's Teeth. The location was hidden and had to be approached from the North.

"How did you find out about this place?" I asked Rose as we closed in on the training facility. "There's nothing out here."

"This is deep in hellion territory," Rose answered. "Hellions know what happens on their land, even if they act like they don't. The Company bought this plot from House Rage several years ago and then tried to close it off."

"Close it off?" I asked. "How could they close it off?"

"Traps and neutralizers were scattered at the perimeter of their property," Rose answered. "This meant The Company had something to hide. Something big enough they felt the need to go far into hellion territory. So I did some digging and found this place."

She pointed to the compound up ahead.

The Killbox.

The main building was a rectangular, squat, windowless structure about three stories tall and several hundred feet wide. Fenced off around it, I could see an outdoor training ground, a firing range, and obstacle courses. It was designed to prep a large group of soldiers for combat.

We parked the vehicles outside, some distance from the Killbox. I didn't want to take any chances with Lowell, remembering Emissary Sinclair's estate and the mage's habit for placing immolation circles everywhere.

We got out of our vehicles and approached the building carefully. The only entrance I could see was a large door made of solid steel. Embedded into the brick next to the door was a numeric panel.

"Form up," I said, drawing everyone close with a wave. "Rose and I will go after Lowell. The rest of you will deal with the combat security and run interference. They have a barracks below the main structure. Expect trap doors, staircases, and concealed methods of approach."

"Do we know how many security personnel are down there?" Silk asked. "What are we running into?"

"Judging from the size of the structure," Graffon began, "and the limitations of the environment requiring a substantial plumbing system to meet the water demand, my estimation is this structure can house about fifty personnel before it's resources are taxed beyond optimum performance."

We all stared at her.

"Really, Graffon?" Rose said, shaking her head. "Your brain is a damn scary place."

Graffon nodded. "Just an observation."

"Nimble's estimate was between twenty and thirty," I said, "but I would say Graffon is right. We're probably looking at closer to fifty guards here."

"*Six* of us against fifty security personnel?" Silk said and everyone smiled. I was truly dealing with a warped group of officers. "That's all?"

Rose let out a sad sigh. "I almost feel sorry for them."

As strong as they were, I didn't know my team's capabilities in a live battle. We hadn't had an opportunity to train together, which meant I had no idea how this group operated in a combat setting. Rose and I had run into and devastated the security personnel in the Tower, so I knew her abilities, but I was still in the dark on the rest of them. I figured if they were smart and covered each other they could handle this.

It was time to fly or die.

Lowell was an unknown quantity, and out of the six of us, a hellion and a dragon stood the best chance against a psychotic fire mage.

"This is a guerrilla-warfare situation," I declared, keeping my face and tone serious. "You get in, attack, and move back. Keep moving and don't engage in full frontal confrontations. If you do, you'll get overrun."

"So we should only attack from the back, Chief?" Silk asked.

I nodded. "Rear surprise attacks are best," I said. "Good observation, Silk."

"And our formations?" Butch asked. "Wide or tight?"

"Since we'll be moving in pairs," I answered, "we should keep them tight. That will be the most effective."

"Just to recap, Chief," Silk said. "You want us to surprise attack them from the rear and keep it tight?"

"I just said that," I exclaimed, confused why he would repeat what we had just established. "Why are you..." I paused at seeing all their grins. "You know what? Fuck all of you."

They burst out into laughter.

"I was just asking," Silk started between guffaws, "because I was checking my gear, and I didn't see any lube."

More laughter.

"Fucking hilarious," I said, chuckling in spite of myself. "Lock and load. Check your six and keep each other alive. Rose, punch in the code and let's get this bastard."

I scaled up, drew Butterfly and Vaporizer—the hellion shotgun Tam had given me to replace Pinky. Rose stepped up to the numeric panel and tapped in the code. We fanned out to either side of the door in case it was rigged with one of Lowell's exploding circles.

For a few seconds nothing happened. Then the door clicked open.

This was too easy.

"Coms from now on," I commanded on the group channel, bypassing a call into Rowena. *"Lieutenant, I'll take point. Opening that door was too damn easy and it's making me itchy."*

"Was just thinking the same thing," Rose agreed.

"That it was too easy?" I asked.

"No, that you should take point. I don't have scales, and if this door explodes, we could keep testing your tolerances. I know it's not a rocket, but it's still good to learn if your scales keep you from blowing to bits or not."

"Your concern warms me all over," I groaned. *"Once inside, PPD 2 and 3 engage security personnel only. If you get eyes on Mage Lowell, you give PPD 1 his twenty, but do not engage. Copy?"*

They nodded.

I pushed open the door and peeked in fast.

After a few seconds, I stepped in with the team behind me.

Once we all entered, the door slammed shut behind us, locking in place, and klaxons started screaming.

"That's more like it," Rose said with her smile of destruction. *"Let's go find this fucker."*

"Hold your position," I told her. *"Everyone needs to acclimate to the light level."*

As a dragon, my eyes adjusted immediately. I knew hellions were similar in their luminosity response. I didn't know if the rest of the team could respond as fast or what their tattoos enhanced.

"PPD 2 is going right," Graffon said, peeling off to the side with Doe.

"PPD 3 is taking left," Silk said as he and Butch slid to the side and then headed past a small structure.

Rose and I remained at the door, taking in the interior.

Inside, the Killbox was set up similarly to the outside obstacle course.

There were plenty of small structures to mimic

locations for hard breaches. Off to the side, I saw parked vehicles to simulate vehicle attacks and take overs.

The interior looked like a small town. A small town that was going to be full of angry, armed, combat security in a few seconds.

Motion caught my eye and I looked up.

Small turrets sat slowly rotating on the tops of some of the buildings. They weren't tracking the teams, but I had a feeling that was going to change soon.

"Tracking turrets on the buildings," I said over the connector. *"They seem dormant for now, but keep your eyes open."*

"Got them, Chief," Graffon said. *"It would appear they are situated at choke points. If we avoid certain areas we can avoid the majority of them."*

"Good plan," I answered. *"Do not let yourselves be drawn into any dead-end choke points. I'm pretty sure we'll meet whoever is here soon."*

"So the chief wants us to give them a tight rear attack, but avoid choking," Silk shared with a giggle. *"Sounds like he's experienced."*

"Phrasing," Butch added. *"Wait, what if you don't have a gag reflex? Then you can't choke, right?"*

"Both of you shut the hell up before I shoot you myself," Rose snapped. *"Focus on the mission or I'll choke you both."*

"She sounds so hot when she gets violent," Silk answered. *"Promise you'll use the cuffs?"*

Rose rolled her eyes and shook her head in defeat.

Those two were beyond help.

My senses picked up the subtle energy shift behind us. I shoved Rose forward and away from the door.

"What the hell, Chief?" she yelled. "Excuse me works too, you know?"

"Move!" I said, backpedaling away from the large steel door.

I looked closer and saw a large circle design on the door's surface begin to glow orange.

"Shit," Rose said as we turned and ran.

We were ten feet away when it exploded, sending us flying.

CHAPTER 40

*G*unfire erupted all around us. The turrets, which had been dormant when it came to firing up until then, had suddenly decided we were excellent targets.

"*Lowell is so dead,*" Rose snarled, getting to her feet and taking cover from the turrets.

"*Turrets are now active,*" I barked. "*Repeat, turrets are active. Also, look out for circles on a delay. We just avoided one on the front door.*"

"*Roger,*" both teams answered back.

"*We have company,*" Graffon announced. "*Security personnel engaged on South wall. They have ingress from trap doors and hidden staircases.*"

"*Take them down,*" I commanded. "*Lethal force is authorized, but non-lethal if you can manage it.*"

Gunfire erupted all over the Killbox. I had a feeling the non-lethal option was being taken as a suggestion.

"Lowell isn't getting the non-lethal option," Rose stated aloud, looking at me. "He dies *today.*"

I nodded. I would still try and bring Lowell in if I could, but the odds were low that was going to happen.

"We need to find him first," I said aiming and taking down a turret.

"If you would stop playing shoot-the-turret," Rose snapped, "and—oh, I don't know—use your dragon senses and locate the batshit mage in the building with a magical energy signature, maybe that would be more helpful?"

"Cover me," I commanded and closed my eyes. "This isn't as easy as I make it look."

I calmed my breathing and pushed out the noise of guns, people yelling, and turrets firing. The smells of gunpowder, smoke, and fear were moved from my conscious mind—and I listened.

I snapped my eyes open.

"Found him?" she asked. "Where?"

"North side," I said, pointing to the other side of the Killbox. "He's waiting for us."

"Good," she said with a snear. "Let's not disappoint."

"Lowell is on the North side of the Killbox," I announced over the group channel. *"Keep the security occupied on the South side. Stay alert in case we need backup."*

"Just FYI," Rose said aloud as we made our way to the other side of the Killbox, avoiding the turrets, "that dragon bloodhound thing you do is impressive, but it makes you look like you're dealing with a bout of constipation. You may want to work on that, Mr. 'this isn't as easy as I make it look.'"

I shook my head and ignored her, keeping my senses expanded in case Lowell had placed circles around his position. I had a feeling he wouldn't since he would've had to worry about The Company security personnel triggering his traps in addition to us.

The North side was a wide-open expanse covered in more vehicles, large orange cones, and concrete obstacles. It was a driving course designed to train personnel in defensive and aggressive driving.

On the far side of the course stood a figure. His hands burst into flame the moment he saw us.

"Hello, Rose," the figure called out. "You look amazing as usual."

"Fuck you, Lowell," Rose shot back. "You tried to dust us—twice."

Lowell wore a long black coat with silver accents. His black hair was cut short and his dark eyes focused intently on us. Honestly, it was hard to pay attention to anything other than the two fireballs he held in his hands.

"It wasn't personal," he replied with a shrug. "It was really meant for the new chief. You would've been, what do they call it...collateral damage?"

"This was part of the funeral party?" I asked.

He gave me a look of complete distaste.

"Are you really that stupid? Does this look like a funeral party to you?"

"Never been to one, so I couldn't say," I answered as both he and Rose stared at me. "Anyway, you're under arrest for the deaths of Henry Mal, Emissary Sinclair Mal, all of his staff, and also for the attempted murder of two PPD officers."

"Are you serious?" Lowell laughed in disbelief. "Do you know who I work for?"

"He's serious," Rose said, nodding. "That's probably

your one and only chance of walking away from this alive."

"No one is above the law," I said, drawing both guns. "Will you comply?"

He roared and swung his hand.

I leapt to the side as a fireball raced at me and exploded on the ground where I'd been standing. I took cover behind a vehicle next to Rose.

"Guessing that's a *no*, Chief," Rose said. "Can I make him dead now?"

"Dust his ass," I said, firing over the car.

CHAPTER 41

The second explosion caught me by surprise.

The only thing that saved my life was the fact that my scales can react to intense stress reflexively... kind of like Leon's stress erections, but far less embarrassing.

The car we had taken cover behind erupted in a wall of flame as we triggered the circle Lowell had placed on it. Scales covered my body completely now as I was thrown across the driving course, bouncing for several feet, and sliding for ten more. Rose landed a few feet away with a groan.

I expanded my senses and looked at the driving course. It was covered in circles. Every vehicle, obstacle, and open patch of ground had some kind of marking or symbol.

We had walked into a death trap.

"Rose," Lowell said with a shake of his head, "I expected the dragon to be stupid enough to fall for this, but I thought at least you would know better."

Rose shook her head and got to her knees.

"I'm going to end you here, you prick," she growled, removing the vial Pytha gave her from a pocket.

She broke off the seal and drank the dark liquid.

An instant later, she roared as her skin changed.

The only way to describe it was her skin turned to—scales. The nails of her hands elongated and became claws. Her teeth transformed to fangs and her eyes gave off an orange glow.

"Rose," I said tentatively, "you still here?"

She whirled her head in my direction and snarled. I stood absolutely still as she refocused on Lowell.

"Time to die, Mage," she raged in a guttural voice and leapt.

Lowell fired several fireballs in our direction. I rolled to the side dodging them as Rose closed the distance.

"Are you mad?" Lowell screamed toward me as he ducked behind a car. A few seconds later, he rolled and ran as it exploded. "You gave her dragon feralmones?"

"I didn't give her anything!" I argued, firing Butterfly and hitting him in the arm.

He spun around and unleashed a wave of fire in my direction. I ducked behind a concrete obstacle and saw the glowing circle materialize under my boots.

"Fuck me," I said, pressing Whoosh and forming my wings.

The explosion launched me into the air.

Momentarily disoriented, I shook my head to clear it, just in time to catch a pair of fireballs in the face.

"Stay back, you bitch," I heard Lowell yell as he retreated. "Get away from me!"

I landed with a thud.

My wings retracted and I half-expected another circle to materialize under me. When nothing happened, I realized that Lowell must have been controlling the detonation of the circles somehow.

Right now, all his focus was on Feral Rose, and staying alive.

Rose took a fireball to the chest and shrugged it off like it was nothing.

Lowell was in deep shit.

"Rose," I called over the connector, *"can you hear me? Come back, Lieutenant."*

She paused for a second, shook her head, and jumped at Lowell. He tried to dive to the side, but Rose was too fast. She caught him mid-leap and raked a hand across his chest.

Lowell crumbled to the ground panting.

Whatever material his coat was made of shredded like tissue paper.

Her razor sharp claws went through it, Lowell's skin, bone, and muscle in one easy swipe.

"Fuck you, Rose," Lowell hissed as he grunted in pain. "You both can go to hell."

Rose half-screamed and roared as she stood over Lowell.

I was beginning to understand that my second-in-command had some serious anger issues.

She jumped back and landed in a crouch.

Lowell formed another fireball and launched it at her. She dodged it, closed the distance, and swiped his throat.

His neck couldn't resist those claws, and so his head rolled across the driving course.

Feral Rose then focused on me.

"Fuck," I said holding my hands in front of my body. "Rose, it's me...the chief."

Another snarl as she closed the distance. I formed my wings.

"Guys," I said on the group channel, *"we have a problem."*

"Yeah like a bunch of assholes trying to kill us?" Silk answered. *"Kind of have our hands full here, Chief."*

The glow in Rose's eyes intensified. I needed to hit her with something hard enough to break through the mindless effect of the feralmones.

That's when Lowell's circles started to glow.

"Holy shit," I said, muttering to myself. I made sure to keep my distance from Rose as I glanced around. "Lowell was one insane mage prick."

He must have set the circles to go off all at once in case we took him down.

"I want you all to evacuate—now!" I commanded over the group channel. *"Now! Lowell set this entire place to blow. Get the fuck out of the Killbox!"*

"What about you and the lieutenant, Chief?" Graffon asked. *"We can't leave—"*

"Get out now!" I yelled. *"That's an order!"*

I had an idea, but it was shaky.

If I missed the timing, not even my scales would protect me from this inferno. The circles began glowing brighter as I closed the distance on Rose.

"You wanted to test tolerances, Rose," I said under my breath. "Well, this is going to be an ultimate field test."

"Kill dragon," Rose said with a rasp, raking her claws across one of the concrete obstacles. "Kill."

"Come get me, hellion."

$\mathcal{I}$ had to wait for the first circle to detonate.

The explosion started a chain reaction as Rose lunged, but it wasn't a large enough explosion. I dodged to the side and punched her in the face.

It would have been softer punching one of the concrete obstacles.

My fist rocked her head back slightly. Sparks flew as her claws raked across the surface of my arm gouging out valleys of pain in my scales. I drove an elbow into the side of her head, which spun her around.

She used the momentum of the elbow strike to lash out with a back kick into my abdomen. I doubled over. When she attempted to smash my head like a melon with a hammer fist, though, I slipped around her, formed my wings and grabbed her from behind. With two quick pumps of my them, we were airborne.

She thrashed in my arms but couldn't break my grip. Her mindless state gave her strength, but thankfully, it wasn't focused.

I saw a cluster of circles together in the center of the driving course. Lines ran from these circles to all the others.

A nexus point, just what I needed.

I dive-bombed for the cluster of circles as it grew brighter. If I got the timing wrong, we would land hard and Rose would shred me with her claws. I needed to make sure I didn't miss.

As we drew closer to Lowell's spells, I released as much dragon energy as possible.

Part of me began to think saving this hellion was a waste of time.

I shut that down as best as I could and headed for the circles. I was about a foot away when they went off.

Rose took the full blast in her face.

The initial explosion launched us into the ceiling with force. I was slightly dazed from the impact when we landed and rolled.

"Chief," Rose asked with a groan a few seconds later, "what the fuck happened?" She pushed up on an elbow and scanned the area, slowly returning to look like her normal self. "Where's Lowell?"

I saw the lines connecting to the other circles increase in brightness and wrapped my wings around us both.

We didn't have time to get out.

"Remember when you wanted to do that field test?" I asked quickly. "Here it comes."

"What are you talking about?" she asked looking around. "Oh. Fuck me...this is—"

All of the circles detonated.

We was shot up so high that I remembered seeing the Dragons Teeth Mountains in the distance, just as I lost consciousness.

CHAPTER 43

The next face I saw belonged to Tam. I was in some kind of medical facility. Tam looked down at me, glanced at her watch, and made a notation on a clipboard.

Yarrl walked over with a smile.

"We can discharge him in a few hours," Tam said. "It appears dragons, like hellions, are fairly resistant to damage. Shame they aren't very intelligent."

Yarrl leaned over and checked some of the charts hanging near my bed. I looked up and saw Rose in a bed similar to mine. Tam was checking up on her the same way she had done with me moments earlier.

"Where are we?" I asked around the headache that was trying to split my head in two. "Is this PPD HQ?"

Yarrl shook his head. "This is Badlands Medical. Not far from The Morgue."

"My team—?"

"Is fine," Yarrl answered, pressing my chest back and

keeping me in the bed. "They evacuated when you told them to. They'll swing by later before you're discharged."

"What about the Lieutenant?" I asked. "We were in a bad explosion."

"So I hear," Yarrl said looking over to where Rose slept. "All I can say is that it's a good thing she's a hellion. Don't know if anyone else, besides a dragon, would have made it out of there in one piece."

"The Killbox?"

"The training facility run by The Company was disintegrated," Yarrl answered. "There's nothing left of the Killbox."

"What do you mean disintegrated?" I asked. "Lowell had only set circles—"

"In the *entire* facility," Yarrl finished. "No one was supposed to leave that place alive—no one. You and your team are the only ones who made it out. You saved their lives, telling them to get out when you did."

I laid my head back in the bed and closed my eyes. In the back of my mind, there were some nagging questions.

How did those circles go off after Lowell died?

Did Masters have some way of controlling them?

What if Lowell hadn't placed all of those circles?

I'd have to deal with that later. Now, I was going to do something I hadn't done since I became chief.

Get a few good hours of sleep.

CHAPTER 44

J looked around the table and motioned to Percy for another round of blood ale.

"Then the chief squealed, *'Get out now!,'*" Silk continued. "I thought he wanted some alone time with Rose. Next thing I know the whole place is exploding. Talk about banging!"

I groaned and hid my face.

"Actually," Graffon started to a group groan, "this only proves my theories—which are backed up by real statistics and hard data, mind you—that having a dragon chief only increases the likelihood of massive destruction in proximity to said chief. The data, which is quite riveting, shows—"

"Ugh," Butch said lifting a flagon to his lips. "Enough, Graffon. You're killing us." He slammed the booze back and winced. "We get it. You get excited with data."

Graffon blushed.

"It's not that exactly...I mean, I do find data fascinating. It's not excitement, per se."

The table erupted with more laughter.

I went over to the bar to clear the tab.

"Your money's no good here, Chief," Percy said, pushing my hand back. "Badlands PPD can always drink on the house, at least while I'm still running the joint."

"Thanks," I said looking back at the table. "My team is insane."

"Only way it works in Infernal City," Percy chuckled as he cleaned a glass. "Glad you found the person who launched a hellion through my window?"

I nodded. "I am, but I know he was working for someone else."

"Usually the case," Percy agreed. "Cut off one head, two grow back."

"I'm just glad the funeral party's done," I said. "I'm tired of trying to deal with that nonsense."

Percy nodded.

"At least now you only have to deal with run-of-the-mill assassination attempts," he said with a smile. "Must be a load off your shoulders."

"The fuck?" I replied, surprised. "What are you talking about?"

"The funeral party is like the introduction to your new life, however short it may be. Fact is, PPD chiefs are targeted throughout their careers in this lovely land of ours. Why do you think the turnover rate is so high?"

So that was it, huh? My destiny was to try and stop the bad guys while a target remained on my back.

Yay.

I glanced back at my crew. They seemed decent

enough, once you got past their irreverence and tinges of psychopathy.

Besides, it wasn't like I was going to go back and tell Hilda that I was uncomfortable doing this job. Even the *thought* of telling my valkyrie mother about my discomfort made me shiver. The way she expressed disappointment was often terrifying, and that's coming from a guy who just lived through a lot of shit over the last few days. No, Hilda would only hear that I was going to stay and do my damnedest to clean up this town. Anything less would result in me learning some new 'lessons.'

No, no, no.

I was still uncircumcised and I intended to stay that way.

"I think I'm going to need another blood ale," I said with a sigh.

Percy placed a large glass of warm booze on the bar next to me and put a massive hand on my shoulder.

"Welcome to the Badlands PPD, Chief Phoenix," he said with a laugh. "It only gets worse from here."

∼

The End

∼

Thanks for Reading
If you enjoyed this book, would you **please leave a review** at the site you purchased it from? It doesn't have to be a book report... just a line or two would be fantastic and it would really help us out!

John P. Logsdon
www.JohnPLogsdon.com

John was raised in the MD/VA/DC area. Growing up, John had a steady interest in writing stories, playing music, and tinkering with computers. He spent over 20 years working in the video games industry where he acted as designer, programmer, and producer on many online games. He's now a full-time comedy author focusing on urban fantasy, science fiction, fantasy, Arthurian, and GameLit. His books are racy, crazy, contain adult themes and language, are filled with innuendo, and are loaded with snark. His motto is that he writes stories for mature adults who harbor seriously immature thoughts.

Orlando A. Sanchez
www.orlandoasanchez.com

Orlando has been writing ever since his teens when he was immersed in creating scenarios for playing Dungeons and Dragons with his friends every weekend. The worlds of his books are urban settings with a twist of the paranormal lurking just behind the scenes and generous doses of magic, martial arts, and mayhem. He currently resides in Queens, NY with his wife and children and can often be found lurking in the local coffee shops where most of his writing is done.

CRIMSON MYTH PRESS

Crimson Myth Press offers more books by this author as well as books from a few other hand-picked authors. From science fiction & fantasy to adventure & mystery, we bring the best stories for adults and kids alike.

www.CrimsonMyth.com

Made in the USA
Coppell, TX
25 May 2021